Perfectly
Innocent

PERFECTLY INNOCENT

Tamra Lassiter

This is a work of fiction. Certain real locations are mentioned, however all names, characters, events and incidents described in this book are fictitious or a product of the author's imagination. Any resemblance to real persons, living or deceased, is entirely coincidental.

PERFECTLY INNOCENT

ISBN-13: 978-0-9899436-8-0 (trade paperback)
ISBN-13: 978-0-9899436-9-7 (e-book)

www.tamralassiter.com

For my sister, Rachel.
LYLTWB

Also by Tamra Lassiter

Something to Lose

Favorable Consequences

I Take Thee to Deceive

Chapter One

Phoebe

My spine stiffens.

I thought that I'd imagined the sound, but there it is again. A muffled gurgle...maybe. Then silence.

Not a sound that belongs in my home.

I think of fleeing.

I can't.

The urge to see where it's coming from is too great. Besides, it doesn't sound threatening. How stupid would I feel if I called someone to help me, and it was just the dishwasher overflowing or something equally frightening?

I breathe in deeply, taking my fortification from the air around me, and then release it slowly. My heartbeat echoes in my ears.

I take my first steps, moving gingerly toward the

back of the house. Goosebumps wash over my arms.

The sound echoes again.

Why am I being so ridiculous? Get your butt in there and see what the problem is.

It probably isn't even that loud, anyway. It just seems that way because it doesn't belong. I expel a breath and get on with it. My courage renewed, I ignore the bumps of warning on my arms, take the turn into the kitchen...and fall to my knees.

Hysteria bubbles to the surface of my being.

My breaths now escape as rough sobs.

A black cloud forms around my vision, but I push it away as I try to assess the sight before me.

There's blood—*so much blood*—in pools and smears on my white floor.

And a man.

Just lying there.

Bleeding.

Something protruding from his chest.

I choke back the bile that's building in my throat. It's too late to turn back. I crawl to him slowly on shaky limbs. I sway, dizzy from the sight before me.

His chest rises and falls, revealing the source of the sound.

Is he alive?

I lean over him, careful not to touch any of the blood, and study his eyes. Glassy, but then he blinks.

He's alive. Seems impossible, but it's real.

Another deep breath. Not a good thing because with it comes the sickening smell of blood. *Do not pass out.*

My phone. I need my phone. My purse is on the floor where I fell. I attempt to stand, but my legs give out beneath me. I lunge toward my purse, feeling successful when I grip the soft leather in my hand.

My fingers feel like they belong to someone else, heavy and difficult to move. I concentrate and manage to dial.

He takes another ragged breath. I slide back toward him in some type of demented army crawl as the call connects.

"9-1-1. What is your emergency?" It's a simple question. My answer comes out in uneven breaths, garbled even to me, and I know what I'm trying to say. How do I even begin?

"Are you hurt?"

"N-n-n-o. But he is."

"I'm sending help now." *They'll never make it in time.*

"On floor. Knife." I'm trying to make sense, but my thoughts come in dribs and drabs. My brain is working overtime to process what has happened. There's no space left to process talking.

I'm leaning over him again. Do I know him? I struggle to remember, too flustered to think.

His eyes connect with mine as he takes another gurgled breath. The hilt of the knife moves up and down with the erratic movement of his chest.

"Stay with me," the operator says. "Help will arrive in a few minutes. Can you tell me your name?"

My attention stays focused on the man and his light brown eyes. He knows that I'm here. He lifts his hand and reaches toward me. I take it in my own and scoot closer to him, feeling the wetness of his blood. I know that I shouldn't touch him, but how can I not? He's going to die before help arrives, and he can't die alone.

"Ma'am. Are you there?"

"Yeah," I answer quietly.

"What is your name?"

"Phoebe. Phoebe Little...I mean Davidson. It's Phoebe Davidson."

His chest rises and falls. His lips move once and then again. Is he trying to speak? I lean closer until my ear is right over his mouth just in time to hear his last dying breath.

Chapter Two

Logan

It never gets any easier.

I chose to be a detective so that I could help put away the worst of the worst, but it leaves a mark and from the sounds of things, this case is going to be one that I'll never forget. Officer Fuller warned us that this crime scene is particularly gruesome. I sit in the car for an extra moment to steel my nerves. If Fuller thought to give me a warning, then it must be bad.

I exit my car and take in the scene outside. The air is warm and thick enough that I can almost feel it as I walk toward the house. This is a nice area, not one where you would expect a crime of this magnitude. The houses are small but well-maintained as are the yards. From what I can see on this dark night, nothing is out of place. Well, nothing except for the two police cruisers and the ambulance that's now leaving the scene. Pulling away with no lights, no siren, and no body inside. There's no need—I already know that the victim didn't make it.

Fuller meets me as I get to the door. He's young and eager to please, but he's an okay guy. He's been one of the nicest men I've met so far and definitely the most welcoming cop on the force. There's always politics in any precinct, but I'd hoped that when I transferred from the craziness of Miami to tiny Hickory Grove, Virginia I'd be getting away from all that. Nope. Instead, I landed in a whole ration of shit when I got the job that one of the locals had his eye on. Seems as if my new partner, Swann, had his hopes on one of his best buds getting the job. The fact that Officer Mason doesn't have enough experience to be a detective—well, that isn't a factor for either of them.

I should have figured out that running away from my problems wasn't the answer. First, I ran to Miami to escape my asshole father. Then, I ran here to escape the assholes working at my precinct in Miami. Now, I'm working with assholes here. Maybe there are assholes everywhere, and there is no escape.

I put all my personal problems away and concentrate on Fuller, the yellow light from the porch lending a green tint to his skin.

"How bad is it?"

"It's the worst thing I've ever seen." He takes a deep breath. "I came out to get some fresh air."

I was briefed on my way over, so I know the basics of the case. Woman comes home to find a dead body in her kitchen, bleeding out. Multiple stab wounds.

"How's the woman who found him?"

"A mess. She's right inside."

I take a long, deep pull of fresh air into my lungs and then follow Swann into the house. The smell is the first thing to hit me. The metallic stench attacks my nose full force. I swallow hard. I've seen a couple of stabbings before—two to be exact, but they were both outdoors, where the odor of death could dissipate. That isn't the case in this cozy, little house.

A woman sits alone on the couch, huddled under a blanket. She stares blankly at the space in front of her, blue eyes wide. It's an easy deduction that she's the one who found the body. Very long, straight brown hair, the tips of which are darker. As I get closer, I see that they're covered in blood.

"I'm Detective Logan Matthews," I say, extending my hand toward her.

"Phoebe Davidson." A shaky hand moves to meet mine. Her pale skin is smeared with blood, so I pull mine away and watch as hers falls to her lap. The blank look on her face doesn't change.

"Ms. Davidson, you found the victim?" A slight nod is her only response. "Do you know him?"

"Un uh."

"One moment please." I attempt a smile and move toward the kitchen. There is only a small dining area that separates the rooms, but the layout of the home is such that the kitchen is around a corner and can't be seen from the living room. That is probably why Ms. Davidson is sitting in the other room.

Swann stands in the dining area with three uniformed officers. All are white-faced and speaking in hushed tones. I walk toward them. Nothing that Fuller told me could have prepared me for the sight that greets me. I catch myself and swallow hard to keep from heaving the greasy burger I ate for dinner.

The D.B. is male, Caucasian, looks to be around forty years old. Dark hair infused with a bit of grey, dark eyes that stare vacantly at the ceiling. The hilt of what appears to be a knife protrudes from his abdomen. Blood has pooled on the floor on both sides of the body; some of it has been smeared and is already thickening.

I gather my thoughts and turn toward the nearby policemen. "Who was the first on the scene?"

"Me and Fuller." The words are spoken by Fuller's partner, Officer Brown. I've spoken with Brown a couple of times in my short two weeks here on staff. He's older than I am, somewhere in his forties. He strikes me as a family man, someone who wants to do his job and then go home and do his best to forget it when he's off the clock. He isn't as friendly as Fuller, but he isn't as stand-offish as some of the others either.

"Where was Ms. Davidson when you arrived?"

"She was kneeling there, next to the body." Brown points to the right of the deceased where one of the blood pools has been disturbed, leaving a smear.

"Did anyone process Ms. Davidson?"

"No. That is for the detectives and the medical examiner," Brown replies with a sneer.

I sigh heavily, knowing that would be his answer.

"So, who thought that it would be a good idea for Ms. Davidson to sit on her couch and cover herself in a blanket? Did they not teach you all how to secure a crime scene?"

Brown and the other two officers share an *Oh shit* moment. I know that they know this. We *all* know this. I don't want to cause waves with some of the only people who have been civil to me since I started this job, but what the hell can I do about it? Swann glares at me. He opens his mouth to say something but then thinks better of it. He can't chastise me about this because he knows I'm right.

Brown and the others begin uttering apologies. I wave them all off and ask them to wait outside. We don't need every policeman in town in here sightseeing and getting their DNA all over the place. They trudge out the door as the medical examiner, Dr. Frank Garfield, arrives.

I met Frank my first day on the job. I've had

enough experience with the M.E. back home to appreciate the fact that Frank is seasoned. He's in his fifties and has been working this job for most of his career.

"This is Dr. Meera Johnson, our forensic pathologist," Frank says by way of introduction. I shake hands with the woman next to him. She seems to be close to my age, early thirties, with caramel skin. Her dark hair is pulled into a ponytail, revealing a thin face. She smiles and gives me a curt nod.

"Right this way," I say as I turn and walk with them to the kitchen. The sight of the body has an effect on them as well.

***

Frank begins working with the deceased while the rest of us walk back over to the witness.

"Ms. Davidson," I say quietly, breaking her out of her trance. "This is my partner, Detective Swann, and this is Dr. Johnson." She looks at each of us. "Is it okay if we talk to you for a few minutes? We also need to gather some evidence."

She nods but then sets her stare straight ahead.

I put a gloved hand on her shoulder. "Ms. Davidson?"

"Yes. Sorry," she says quickly and stands before us.

"Why don't you let us gather our evidence, and

then you can get cleaned up, okay?"

"What do you need me to do?"

"First, we're going to take some pictures of you. Would that be okay?"

"Yeah."

Dr. Johnson snaps a few pictures, but other than the blood on her hair, there isn't much to see.

"Can we put your blanket in this bag?" I ask, holding a large evidence bag in front of me.

Another nod as she unwraps the covering from her body. I swallow my gasp and hold tight to the blanket as it's released. The blood has soaked and dried into her pants and her hands. There's so much of it that I immediately look for wounds on her body. Dr. Johnson begins snapping photos in rapid succession.

"Are you hurt, Ms. Davidson?" Swann beats me to the question.

"No. This is all from *him*." Tears begin to fall.

Chapter Three

Phoebe

Detective Logan's eyes are a chocolate brown, and most importantly, they're very kind. Detective Swann seems removed, like he would rather be anywhere else. *Who wouldn't?* The doctor is all business. Her light brown eyes show determination. To do a good job? To get her job done and get out of here? Who knows? Detective Logan is the only one showing any care for me and all that I'm going through here. I don't mean to whine—I know that the guy in the kitchen has had it much worse than I have—but Detective Logan is the only one who came to check on me *before* going to see the spectacle in my kitchen.

"I'm sorry to put you through this, but we do need to get whatever evidence we can from you."

"Okay," I say quietly. I'm not sure what that means, but it doesn't sound fun.

"Dr. Johnson will accompany you into your bathroom and process you there. After that, you can take a shower and get cleaned up." A shower would be nice. I want to feel warm. "Is there someone that we can call for you? Maybe a family member?"

I dictate my sister's phone number. I figure that is probably standard procedure for this kind of thing, but Detective Logan is still the one who asked.

"Please don't let her see him," I say softly. He nods.

"When you return, we'll have some questions for you." That comes from Detective Swann.

I search for the kind eyes again. "Detective Logan, thank you for calling my sister." *And being so nice to me.*

He smiles. "It's Detective Matthews, ma'am. Detective *Logan* Matthews."

"I'm sorry," I say quickly. I feel a blush move up my cheeks. That seems silly with all that has happened, but calling him by his first name makes me feel warm somehow.

"No apology necessary ma'am."

I follow the doctor into my bathroom.

***

Dr. Johnson is a little more personable once we get away from the others, but not much, and the experience on the whole is nothing short of awful. She bags my clothes item by item, snapping pictures along the way like I'm some kind of nude model.

She scrapes under my fingernails and thoroughly inspects my skin, taking things with tweezers that I can barely see. She also gives me a haircut, trimming off the blood-soaked hair. I don't want that hair anymore—I really don't, but I can't stop the tears from streaming down my cheeks at feeling so violated—first my home and now my body. To top it off, I'm fingerprinted so that they can look for fingerprints that are in my home that are not mine. It's just one humiliation after another. By the time I finally get to shower, I'm over all of it.

I want these people out of my house.

I want this all to go away.

I stay in the shower until the water runs clear, turns cold, and I run out of tears. But during this time I've come to a conclusion. What happened here tonight was horrible. Watching that man die in such a gruesome way will live with me until the day I die. I know that the vision of him—*I don't even know his name*—on the floor will stay with me forever. I am a victim here as well. This is not my fault. I did the right thing in staying with him at the end. I never would have forgiven myself if I had walked away from him and he'd had to die alone. I will get over this, and I will get my life back to normal as soon as possible. I can't waste any more of my life getting over *another* traumatic experience. I make that promise to myself. Maybe I need to figure out why horrible things keep happening to me.

I hear the knock as soon as I turn off the water. "Phoebs?" It's Lilly, thank goodness. "I have some clothes for you. Can I come in?"

I quickly wrap the towel around me and give her the okay to come inside. She places a small stack of clothes near the sink and then pulls me to her for a tight hug. My eyes moisten again. Lilly's eyes are already wet with tears.

"You poor thing," she says as she pats my back in consolation. "I just can't imagine." Her words trail off, and she squeezes more tightly.

"Let me get dressed, and I'll be right out."

"Do you need help, or can I get you anything?"

"No. Thank you for being here. I'm sorry to drag you away from Kevin and the girls, but I'm glad you're here." She gives me a weak smile and exits the bathroom.

I dress quickly in the sweatpants, t-shirt, and sweatshirt that Lilly had set on the counter and wipe down the mirror so that I can get a look at my reflection. I know that what I've been through has left a mark on me. I'm almost surprised that I can't literally see it on my face. I run a quick brush through my hair, take a deep breath, and exit the bathroom.

Lilly stands at the end of the hallway. We look so much alike—people have said that since the day I was born. My hair *was* longer than hers before the doctor cut it. Now, we look even more alike. My sister. My best friend. Practically inseparable since birth, well my birth since she's eighteen months older than me. She hooks her arm through mine as I enter my living room and escorts me to the couch. I'm relieved to see that for all the blood that was on the front of my pants, there is none on my couch.

Lilly takes the spot next to me and puts a comforting arm around my shoulders. The scent of sunscreen fills my nose. She took my nieces to the pool tonight.

Detectives Matthews and Swann huddle together in the dining room, conversing quietly. Detective Matthews's eyes meet mine from across the room, and I feel a flutter in my chest. I dismiss it immediately. There is no way that it could be *that kind* of flutter, not when there's a dead man lying in my kitchen.

The detectives walk over to us. I really take notice of them for the first time. Both wear dress slacks and dress shirts. Detective Matthews wears a tie, but Detective Swann wears his collar open at the top. Their similarities end there. Detective Swann is in his fifties, at least. He's on the round side. His cheeks are puffy, his skin pale in contrast to his dark hair. His hair shows no sign of grey, but it does look pretty thin across the top. He will likely be bald in a few years. He makes up for the lack of hair on his head with a large mustache. His deep grey, almost black, eyes study me as well. His lip curls up as if he doesn't like what he sees. His mustache kind of curls in on itself. *So not attractive.*

Detective Swann sits in the chair across from me, leaving Detective Matthews with only one place to sit, next to me. He takes his seat but sits as far away from me as the sofa will allow.

I move my gaze to study him, a much nicer view than Detective Swann, who literally pales in comparison. He looks to be about my age. His skin is tan, and his body is hard. His brown hair is cut short, no grey to be seen there either. His eyes are coffee brown, dark and secretive. He looks to me like he understands me, whereas Detective Swann looks like he's trying to figure out what I'm hiding. I blush under the heat of their stares. *Let's get this over with already.*

Chapter Four

Logan

This poor woman has been through a lot tonight. I almost wish that we could give her some time to rest before hitting her with a bunch of questions. That's not the way it works though, we need her thoughts while they're fresh.

Fresh.

She looks fresh from her shower. Her damp hair falls to her shoulders. I can smell her clean scent from over here.

Strawberries.

Stop thinking about how she smells.

I clear my throat and look at Swann. He nods his okay for us to begin.

"Ms. Davidson." I turn toward her. Her eyes meet mine. No longer comatose, they're intelligent and hopeful. "Can you tell us what happened tonight?"

She folds her hands together in her lap and takes a deep breath. "I had been out to dinner. I came home, and I heard it."

"What time was this?" Swann asks.

"Close to ten."

"What did you hear?"

"A noise. I didn't know what it was at first. I found him lying there." Her eyes widen as she remembers. "There was so much blood. It just seemed surreal, like it couldn't really be happening. It was hard to process what it was." Her sister rubs her back. "I assumed he was dead, but then he breathed."

"He was *alive* when you arrived?" Swann asks, the disbelief evident in his tone. Can't blame him for that. I can hardly believe it myself, and I saw him in there.

Ms. Davidson's eyes remain in her lap. Her head nods slightly. "Yes. He reached his hand out to me, so I leaned down close to him and took it. I guess that's how I got so much...blood...on me." She shivers slightly. "I couldn't let him die alone."

"Did he speak to you?"

"No." Her face curls up in confusion, causing the end of her button-like nose to tip upward. She looks up slowly, and her eyes meet mine again. "He died before the ambulance arrived. I don't know the exact moment that it happened. His breaths were far apart at that point, and then they just eventually stopped all together."

I'm glad that my hands are busy taking notes, because I want to reach out and comfort her myself. Why did she have to go through something so terrible?

Swann continues the questioning. "Do you know the deceased?"

"No. I've never seen him in my life."

"You're sure about that?"

"Yes." The word comes out forcefully, as she turns her gaze back to Swann. Why is he being such an ass?

"Do you have any idea how this man ended up stabbed and in your kitchen?"

Ms. Davidson sits a little straighter. Her sister's hand falls off her back.

"I have no idea how he got there, and I don't know who he is. Is that clear enough for you?"

I need to diffuse this escalation of tempers and right now. I allow my fingertips to touch her shoulder lightly, just enough to get her attention. She turns toward me.

"Ms. Davidson, I'm sorry that we have to go through this now, but it really is important." She nods. She has two tiny freckles under her left eye. *Focus.* "Where were you earlier this evening?" I have to work to keep my tone level.

"I had dinner at Barney's Bar and Grill."

"Were you there alone?"

A blush of pink moves up her neck to her cheeks.

"I had a date. His name is Jeffrey Phillips."

"Was Mr. Phillips with you when you came home this evening?" *Please say no.*

"No. We met at the restaurant and drove home separately."

"What is the extent of your relationship with Mr. Phillips?" I have to ask the question, and I *really* want to know her answer. I've never had this reaction to a witness before. What the hell am I doing?

"It was our first date," she replies shyly, looking down at her lap again. "It was an Internet date through Lovematch.com." Her cheeks redden even more. "But it didn't really work out, so we won't be going out again."

I purse my lips tightly so that they cannot form a smile. This woman is a witness. I shouldn't be concerned with her dating profile. But, I also can't kid myself. There's something about her that makes me want to pull her into my arms and comfort her. *What the hell is wrong with me? Focus you idiot.*

"And Mr. Phillips will be able to corroborate your story?" Swann adds.

She sits straighter again and glares at him. "Is there a reason that I'd *need* him to corroborate my story?"

Damn it, Swann.

"We are just trying to investigate what happened, Ms. Davidson. We have to validate the information that we are presented with."

"You know what? This conversation is over." Her sister speaks clearly, looking at both me and Swann in turn. "You can discuss this further with my sister *and her lawyer.*"

"Lawyer?" Ms. Davidson asks. "Am I in trouble? Do I need a lawyer?"

"No, ma'am," I answer quickly. "We are just trying to figure out what happened."

"If she isn't being charged, then we are leaving now. She will be at my house." Her sister pulls her up and drags her out the front door. Swann curses under his breath.

The look of panic on her face has me ready to punch something. We should be consoling her right now, not scaring her even more.

"What the hell was that all about, Swann? Don't you think you were a little hard on her?"

He stands, looking duly put out, as if this whole conversation is beneath him. "Look Matthews, I don't buy her whole innocent story. Maybe what she says is true, maybe she just sauntered in here and found a man stabbed and bleeding to death on her kitchen floor. But, that doesn't happen without a reason. If she didn't do the deed herself, then she's involved with the kind of people who make those things happen. This *is not* a random act."

Swann's hands are on his hips, his whole body challenging me to disagree with him. *I can't.* He's right. This is not a random act of violence. This guy is dead in her kitchen for a reason, and for the first time in my career, I pray that our only suspect has nothing to do with it.

"Let's get this wrapped up for tonight. It's late enough."

Chapter Five

Phoebe

"Are you sure you'll be okay here by yourself?" Lilly asks me. *Again.* I take a deep breath and release it slowly before turning toward her.

"Lill, please. I will be just fine." It's only been a matter of hours, and yet I've already grown tired of the sympathetic look in her eyes. "I will certainly be okay here long enough for you to take the girls to camp. Just go."

"If you're sure. I won't be gone long, and I'll stop by the store on my way back home." I nod impatiently. This is at least the third time that Lilly has told me her plan. I got it already. She flashes me a quick smile and then turns toward the stairway. "Girls!" she screams too loudly for my ears. "Time to go."

The footsteps come from different directions and then converge at the top of the staircase before they boom-boom-boom down the stairs like a herd of elephants. How can two small creatures make so much noise? Their smiling faces and swooshing braids are evidence that they have no idea that there's anything amiss in their home. They look so much like our side of the family, their brown hair and big blue eyes. Everyone who sees them says they're the spitting image of Lilly and me when we were their age.

They were so happy to see me when they awoke this morning, like I was a gift from the Tooth Fairy or something. At four and five years old, it takes very little to make them happy. We had a nice breakfast together—well, they ate, and I watched them eat— and then Lilly sent them back upstairs to brush their teeth.

Hillary, the oldest, marches right up to me. "Aunt Phoebe?"

"Yes, Pumpkin."

"Will you spend the night with us tonight? We can have a slumber party." Her little eyes brighten at the thought. It's my own fault that Hillary wants a slumber party. I slept over a couple weeks ago, so their parents could go on a date. We made a tent on the living room floor with blankets and carefully placed dining room chairs. I let them stay up until eleven, and we watched movies. I must say, it was the best night *I* have had since Lilly, Mom, and I went to Atlantic City for my birthday in January. It was a different kind of fun, but a blast all the same. Maybe that's why I'm an elementary teacher—on the inside I'm just a big kid. However, fun time aside, I'm not up for that kind of evening right now. I'm still traumatized from last night and am likely to be for a very long time.

I look to Lilly for guidance. She answers for me right away. "Aunt Phoebe is going to be staying with us for a while." Cheers erupt as both Hillary and her sister Madison begin jumping up and down. "So we will save the slumber party for another night." The jumping stops, but the smiles remain.

I hadn't really thought about how long I planned to stay here, but *a while* is too long. I remember the promise that I made to myself last night, and I intend to stick by it. The quickest way to make this nightmare end is to get my life back to normal.

"One more night, I think," I answer quickly. The cheering stops.

"Pl-ease stay longer, Auntie Phoebe." Hillary looks up at me, somehow her eyes are even larger and softer.

"One more night, and then I have to get back home. We will have a sleepover again soon. I promise." The smiles have now been replaced with looks of determination. Hillary and Madison are young, but they know how to manipulate. They haven't given up, and they won't until they eventually get their way.

"We'll talk about it later," Lilly adds sternly, giving me *the look* and not Hillary, before gathering backpacks and lunch boxes and ushering the girls into the garage.

***

When the doorbell rings, I hesitate—not so much because I'm afraid it will be a horde of reporters to question me about last night. *Should I be worried about that?* I just know that I'm not in the mood to talk with anyone. But this is Lilly's house, so I finally drag my butt out of the comfy chair and make my way to the door.

It's Detective Matthews. Detective *Logan* Matthews, and he appears to be alone.

I open the door slowly, not sure what my reaction should be at seeing him here. It probably shouldn't be the tsunami that forms in the pit of my stomach. It whirls and churns and then explodes, taking over everything as a wave of nausea flows through my body. The tidal wave subsides, leaving only the back-and-forth of small, choppy waves that my stomach must somehow navigate. I know that I shouldn't be experiencing any fluttering, but yet it's there. Maybe it is just a nervous reaction to the fact that a policeman is here to see me. That would be understandable, warranted even. When the flutters travel lower, I have to admit to myself that they're for reasons other than his occupation.

He's dressed in charcoal slacks and a bright white dress shirt. No tie today. He didn't shave this morning. The dark stubble on his cheeks looks somehow sexier than a clean shave. That definitely *is not* the case for us girls. The only giveaway that he isn't about to pose on some hot-guy calendar are the dark shadows under his eyes. He looks fresh-from-the-shower delicious, and I'm still dressed in the same sweatpants and t-shirt that he saw me in last night, only now they're wrinkled from sleep. Well, they're wrinkled from tossing and turning. It's not like I actually slept. I realize that he's still standing on the porch studying me, and neither of us has said a word.

"I thought that we weren't supposed to talk without a lawyer present." *Did those words just come out of my mouth?* I grimace internally, maybe externally too. *Way to go, Phoebe. Give him a reason to leave.*

"That's true. We aren't allowed to talk about the case without a lawyer present." Detective Matthews pauses and looks down at his clasped hands. "But I'm not here to talk about the case." His beautiful brown eyes meet mine again. "I really just wanted to make sure that you are okay. You went through so much last night, and well...I've been worried about you."

I feel the corners of my mouth break into a smile. *He's been worried about me.* Is it normal for cops to check up on people? Maybe. Probably. *I hope not.* He smiles back. I place a hand on my stomach to calm the trembling tsunami that is now wreaking havoc on my insides.

"I'm okay, I think."

"Good."

I turn the tables on him. "You look awfully tired. Would you like a cup of coffee?"

"Um." He shifts his feet uncomfortably.

"But you have to promise that we won't talk about the case."

"Scouts honor," he says while making a crisscross motion over his heart.

"Were you really a scout?"

"No," he says with a chuckle.

"Then how do I know I can trust you to keep your word?" *Am I flirting now?*

He stands a little straighter, his face all seriousness. "You can trust me."

I look into his eyes—eyes so open that they seem to be the windows to his soul, and I know that I can trust him. I open the door wide enough for him to enter. He waits just inside until I close it, and we start moving toward the back of the house to the kitchen. Lilly and Kevin's house is much larger than the crackerjack box that I live in. You have to walk through the foyer, a hallway, and then an open space before you get to the large area at the back of the house with the gourmet kitchen, breakfast room, and family room. There's a sunroom and a huge deck with a screened-in porch past that. It's pretty sweet.

I turn to take a peek at Detective Matthews behind me. I fold my hands together and place them both on my stomach. The fluttering inside is quivering at a whole new level. The dizziness causes me to falter just enough that I lose my balance.

Strong arms wrap around me, saving me from a hard hit to the floor. Heat sears my cheeks from the embarrassment of my clumsiness and the feeling of his arms around me. I'm left staring up into his warm eyes, now showing more concern than ever.

"Don't worry. I've got you."

He's got me. My eyes are drawn to his mouth as he speaks. His lips are full and just right there, inches from my own. I swear he catches me looking. *What is wrong with me?* I move to stand up, and he holds me tighter. *Oh gosh.*

"Are you sure you're okay to stand?"

I nod, and he helps me stand straight. His arms fall to his sides.

"Sorry about that. I guess I'm not as okay as I thought I was. I just need more coffee." I nod my head toward the back of the house and fumble a smile. "This way."

We walk to the kitchen without further events or embarrassment on my part. Detective Matthews insists that I take a seat at the table. He looks around and then, finding the coffee pot, pours us each a cup of coffee. He takes the seat across from me.

His eyes move around the room. "Where's your sister? I thought she would be here to take care of you."

"She had to take my nieces to camp. She'll be back soon."

He nods slowly. "You're going to get a lawyer today, right?" His gaze is steady and serious.

"Yes. We have an appointment with him at eleven. Do I *need* a lawyer?"

"I don't think a person would have any long-term use for a lawyer, but it doesn't hurt to be cautious. That is just hypothetically speaking, of course. I'm not talking about your case."

I smile a small smile. "No. Of course you're not."

I look away to my coffee cup, but I feel the heat of his eyes on my face. "Did you get any sleep at all?"

"About twenty whole minutes." *I hope that my face doesn't look like I got twenty minutes of sleep.* "You?"

"About the same. I was only home for about an hour." Was he at my house the rest of the time? I can't ask him, but that's definitely implied. This feels so strained. What else can I say?

"Someone mentioned last night that you recently moved here from Miami?"

"Yeah, only a few weeks ago." Okay. Guess he isn't one for a lot of words.

"What did you do in Miami to get such a dark tan? Or is everyone that tan down there?"

He looks unsure, but he answers. "I spent a lot of time out on my boat. I like to fish."

"Oh. My dad likes to fish, too. There are a lot of

lakes and ponds around here where you can go."

He smiles politely. "That sounds nice, but I tend toward sport fishing. You know sailfish, swordfish, tuna, that kind of thing."

"Oh. Ocean fishing. We're only an hour from the coast. Have you tried it here yet?"

"No, not yet."

Silence breaks out between us. We sit quietly together, avoiding eye contact. Is he working up the courage to tell me something? Is there something he wants to warn me about, and he doesn't know how? Should I ask him? He's made it clear that we aren't supposed to talk about the case, so I can't. But why is he here?

Lilly finds us together, silently sipping our coffee. She says good morning, slips a jumbo pack of Twizzlers on the table in front of me, and then makes an excuse to leave us alone together.

"Candy for breakfast?" Detective Matthews asks, a smile on his lips.

"They're my go-to snack when I'm upset." *Thanks a lot Lill. Couldn't you have put them over on the counter where the hot guy couldn't see the mega pack of candy that I'm about to consume?*

Detective Matthews hops up and declares that he has to get back to work. He announces that he'll show himself out and practically runs to the door.

Lilly takes his seat at the table. "What the heck was that all about?"

"I have no idea."

Chapter Six

Logan

Shit.

I'm a total idiot.

I made excuses to myself to justify that visit. It's true that I was worried about her, but I can't let her know that—at least not *how* worried. I'm investigating this case. The last thing I need to do is chase the only witness we have like a lovesick puppy.

What the hell was that?

What a mistake to visit her. *I almost kissed her.* Can I chalk the experience up to sleep deprivation or being a moron? It's likely both.

Swann is already at the office when I get there, eyeing me over his coffee cup.

Do I look guilty? Better to come clean with him

than to have Ms. Davidson mention my visit.

"Where have you been?" he barks as I take a seat at my desk.

"Where have I been? Give me a break. I barely took time for a shower." He shakes his head. "And, I had a quick visit with Phoebe Davidson."

His head snaps up. "Why would you do that?"

I sit ramrod straight and maintain eye contact—can't give Swann an inch. "I had to do some damage control after last night. She was answering our questions just fine, and then you had to go all *investigator* on her. Now, she's lawyering up. I mean, in the end that's fine since I don't think she did anything wrong, *but* she was cooperating nicely until your *bad cop* attitude got in the way."

"I just asked her a few questions. I haven't even *begun* to be the bad cop yet."

"You should ask questions but with a nicer attitude. If she's telling us the truth, then she's been through a horrible ordeal. You should show some compassion until she gives us a reason to doubt her."

"And you're just so full of compassion," he says, the condescension dripping from his tongue.

"I only want her to cooperate with us. That will make things go a hell of lot better for us all."

Swann's sigh comes out as a growl. "I really can't believe you went to talk with her. Are you fucking stupid?"

"I just asked how she was doing, tried to make it seem like we are concerned about her well-being."

And held her in my arms longer than I needed to. And almost kissed her. Shit, I am fucking stupid.

"Well don't do it again."

"I wouldn't have had to make amends if you hadn't been such an ass to her in the first place."

Swann turns his attention to a file on his desk. Message received. Conversation over.

Fine.

I log into my computer and begin the background check on Ms. Davidson. There was some preliminary info on her last night, but we haven't had time yet for the full intel. A few taps of keys yields what I need.

Phoebe Davidson, married to Alan Little at age twenty-two and then divorced three years later. What else? No children. Received a degree in Elementary Education from James Madison University and currently teaches the fourth grade at Hickory Grove Elementary.

Wait. *Shit.* There's a drug possession charge— marijuana. The charge was dropped, but it still shows in her record. Swann is going to have a field day with this. I have to admit, I never would have pegged her as a drug user. She seems too clean for that, even with the dead body in her kitchen. But, the charge *was dropped*. So maybe she isn't.

The rest of her file yields nothing of interest. A quick investigation of Alan Little shows that he does have a rap sheet, and it's a long one—drug possession, drug trafficking, and petty theft. He was found with marijuana and heroin, lots of heroin. He even did time in prison. No current address for Little. So where is he these days? I jot down more questions for Ms. Davidson on a legal pad and try *not* to think about how her eyes sparkle when she smiles. I also try *not* to imagine how sparkly her eyes might be when she laughs.

Chapter Seven

Phoebe

Peace and quiet is not to be had in Lilly's home. There was a short respite after the girls left for camp, but once Mom arrives, quiet time is clearly over. Mom cycles between blaming the Hickory Grove Police Department for putting me in a position where I need a lawyer and then the thing I hate the most, pitying me. She means well. I know that she does. I keep reminding myself of that fact as her tirade continues, her blue eyes hot with the fire of her rant and then burning with undeniable pity. I can handle a lot of things, but pity is not one of them.

I've been officially divorced now for six years. I learned to hate being pitied during that nightmare— the long looks, the whispers that stopped when I walked into the room. That's what you get when you marry the love of your life, the person you thought you knew so well, and then you find out that you don't know that person at all. I get it, but I've had enough, and I'm not going there again, no matter what the circumstances.

Maybe the nagging feeling that I've had a few times—that I'm being watched—is because *I am* being watched. Mom and Lilly are probably spying on me every chance they get. I know they care about me, but I need to breathe.

I finally escape to the guest room for a break with the excuse that I need to shower and get ready for a meeting with my lawyer. *Meeting with my lawyer*. The thought is so unreal, yet it's sadly not the first time that I've needed a lawyer for something I didn't do. I'm a good person. But the fact remains that good people, *innocent people*, get put in jail sometimes for crimes they didn't commit. It's heartbreaking.

Thank goodness we know a lawyer. Lilly's husband Kevin is best friends with John Jamison, a local attorney who has a great reputation. He helped me out once before when my ex-husband got me into a little trouble. John is a really great guy, and I feel relieved to have him in my corner.

There was a time when Lilly really wished that John and I would hit it off, but we never had any chemistry. She harassed me for months though, constantly listing John's great qualities. I couldn't deny his accomplishments and good taste, but the spark just wasn't there. Turns out that the reason we didn't have a spark was because John has chemistry with his partner, Patrick. Once that little piece of knowledge was out there for the world to see, Lilly finally left me alone.

***

The police station is a scary place, even when it's as small as the one in Hickory Grove. The station uses a converted storefront on Main Street. The first floor has a lobby and a few desks, not sure what else. John and I are directed to take the elevator to the second floor. The door opens to a fairly large area with desks scattered throughout the room. There are a couple of offices in the back. We are escorted to a small room, just to the right of the elevator named Interrogation Room One. That's what the sign says anyway. I don't see Interrogation Room Two, or any others for that matter, nearby.

I feel more comfortable having John with me. Maybe it was a good idea to have a lawyer for this. John's on my side, and it's good to know that someone is. I do feel a little put out that I need a lawyer at all, but I try to think of it as having a very educated friend with me. He looks the part, too. I don't know what an Armani suit looks like, but I can tell that John's suit is a nice one. It's a very dark charcoal, practically black, with a perfectly pressed white shirt, with French cuffs and a power tie. Contrast that with Detective Swann's tight-fitting polyester. *I win.* I wish it was that simple.

I keep telling myself that this is good. Once the police hear my story, they will be able to move forward with their case, and I will be able to move forward with my life. Let's just get this over with already.

For now, though, we sit in Interrogation Room One in hardback wooden chairs that are already feeling uncomfortable, at least mine is. Maybe that's part of the interrogation process. Make the criminals uncomfortable, and they'll be more willing to accept their guilt, a *First World* kind of torture.

We're obviously waiting on something, or maybe we're waiting on a someone since I haven't yet seen Detective Matthews. Detective Swann showed us to this small room and then disappeared.

I take another sip of coffee from the small Styrofoam cup in front of me. I keep drinking coffee in the hopes that it will counteract my lack of sleep from last night, but all it's succeeded in doing is giving me a killer stomach ache.

John stands when the detectives enter. He shakes hands with Detective Matthews and then takes his seat next to me. I watch Detective Matthews as he sits across from me, shuffling through the paperwork he's placed on the table in front of him. He looks the same as he did this morning. I look much better, *but it's not hard considering the total mess I was then.*

I'm wearing a sundress, and I carefully did my hair and make-up. I even got a haircut. It was a cheap haircut, but better than the hack job the police evidence woman did to me last night. It doesn't matter though because Detective Matthews doesn't look at me at all. He continues to shuffle through his file like he's looking for something in particular. Detective Swann speaks, so I have to turn my attention to him.

"Let's go through your story again, Ms. Davidson." He seems nicer than he did last night. His words are straightforward and to the point, but they are trying to find a murderer. I can understand that he doesn't have time for pleasantries. I just don't want him yelling at me like he did the last time we did this.

I summarize the story that I relayed last night, impatiently straightening the skirt of my dress with my hands. "I came home around ten, and there was a man dying on my kitchen floor. He'd been stabbed. I called 9-1-1, but he died before the ambulance arrived."

"Did you know the deceased?"

"No."

"Are you sure?"

John pipes in before I answer. "Detective Swann, my client has clearly stated that she did not know the man. Can we continue?"

I look at Detective Matthews for a little help, but

apparently I'm not going to get any because his head is still stuck in his paperwork. *What is it that he's looking for?* I turn back to Detective Swann.

"If you did not know the victim, then why were you down on the floor with him? If most people found a dead man in their home, they would run to a neighbor. You didn't do that. Instead, you cuddled up to him and made a mess."

I look to John for guidance and he nods. We covered this in his office. "The man was dying. I couldn't just leave him there alone. Plus, I never touched him except for his hand, and I guess my hair. It must have brushed him when I leaned over him. There was blood all over the floor. I couldn't *not* get it on me."

"That is a lot of caring for someone who you *don't know*."

John defends me. "Phoebe is a good person. I've known her for years, and her actions in this regard do not surprise me."

Swann shakes his head and says, "Detective Matthews has something to share."

I turn my attention again to Detective Matthews who looks directly at me. I feel the flutter in my stomach as his eyes meet mine and swallow down the lump that has caught in my throat.

"The deceased has been identified as Ron Carpenter. Does that name mean anything to you?"

I feel all eyes on me as I rack my brain for the name. It doesn't ring a bell or sound familiar in any way.

"No," I say again. "*I don't know him.*"

Detective Matthews's eyes don't falter, but I see something different in them—a flicker of relief maybe, and then he's looking at his paperwork again.

"Ron Carpenter, the drug dealer?" John asks. "Well, I guess I have to say *suspected drug dealer,* since he beats every charge that he's brought up on."

Detective Matthews spits out his answer to John without a look in my direction. "That's the one." John writes a few notes in his notebook and then leans the paper so that I can read what he's written.

Maybe Alan knew him?

I look at John and shrug my shoulders. "I don't know him," I repeat softly for John, but I feel like declaring it from the rooftop.

Detective Swann continues our discussion. "The murder weapon was a knife. The only prints on it were yours, Ms. Davidson."

I gasp. I figured out that the knife was one of mine. I didn't think about it when I was in my house last night, but as I remembered the scene in my mind, which has happened *way* too many times, I see the hilt of the knife. I recognized it at some point during the night as one of the knives from my set. They were a wedding gift. I've explained this to myself, and I will explain it to Detective Swann, but the tone of his voice has the acidic coffee in my stomach churning.

I look at Detective Matthews first. His mouth is slightly open as he stares at Detective Swann. His eyes are pinched.

John pipes up for me. "Mr. Carpenter was stabbed in Ms. Davidson's kitchen with one of her knives. Of course Ms. Davidson's prints would be on the weapon. *It's her knife*. That doesn't mean that she stabbed him. It only means that she took it out of the dishwasher and put it away. The killer was probably wearing gloves." John pauses, seemingly for dramatic effect. "How does this evidence show that Ms. Davidson held the knife?"

"The knife has her index finger and thumbprint," Detective Swann replies.

"Which is exactly how she could have held it when removing it from the dishwasher." John demonstrates with his fingers. I don't know what to say, but I nod. That is how I transfer the sharp knives from the utensil caddy to the knife block that sits on my kitchen counter. "What other questions do you have for my client?" John continues, obviously perturbed.

"Let's discuss how an intruder could have entered your home," Detective Swann continues. "All the doors and windows were locked except for the front door where you say you entered just before finding Mr. Carpenter. Is that correct?"

"I think so. I unlocked the front door when I got

home. I didn't check the rest of the house."

"There were no signs of forced entry, so the murderer had to be someone who has a key."

Chapter Eight

Logan

Ms. Davidson scrunches her forehead, which would be really cute if it wasn't for such a serious reason.

"The only people who have a key to my home are my parents and my sister. I know that they aren't capable of this. There has to be some other way that the killer got in. Maybe he picked the lock?"

"Picking a lock leaves distinctive marks from the tool that was used. The killer did not pick the lock. The windows and doors were locked from the inside. The only remaining explanation is that he or she has a key."

"Well maybe someone stole a key? There has to be some way."

Swann agrees that he will send deputies to

confirm whether or not her parents and her sister are in possession of their copies of the house key. He leaves the room for a moment to set that up. I use the time to study Ms. Davidson. I wish I didn't have to keep calling her that. I've thought about her so many times in the last twelve hours, and truthfully I'm afraid to let myself call her anything other than *Ms. Davidson*. I can't trust myself to not screw up in front of Swann and let on how much I've been thinking of her.

She looks completely worn out, just exhausted. Of course she is. She went through such a horrible ordeal last night and Swann is just making it worse. Bringing up the fingerprints on the knife is ridiculous. We talked about it beforehand, and he agreed. Just like her lawyer said—of course her prints are on the knife.

It's reasonable to ask about the house keys, but Swann is doing it in such a way that makes it sound like he suspects that she stabbed the guy. *Ain't no way.* Can he not see her?

"Would you like some water, Ms. Davidson, or maybe some more coffee?" I find myself asking her. It's the only thing I could come up with to say to her. Plus, I'm the bad guy right now, so anything that I can do for her, I'll do.

"Water would be nice." She almost smiles, but her mouth doesn't quite make it.

I stand and exit the small room, leaving behind her strawberry scent. I'm glad that she has a lawyer here helping her. She shouldn't need one, but at least she has someone looking out for her. It was worth the risk of seeing her this morning to make sure. *I'll just keep telling myself that.*

I was glad to find out that John Jamison has a solid reputation. I was possibly happier, though, to hear that he's gay. I can see that he's an attractive guy and to think about him and *her* working long hours together on this case—let's just say that's something I don't want to think about. It's bad enough that his comment about how he's known her for years just gave me instant heartburn.

She's standing when I return, apparently stretching her legs, so I walk to her side of the table and carefully hand her the cup of water. My fingertips lightly brush hers as I manage the handoff. Electricity shoots up my arm from the contact, causing me to pull away quickly. Her eyes can't hide her surprise. She felt it, too.

Swann returns with a smug look, an expression he wears more often than not. How am I ever going to work with him? He's such an asshole. We all return to our seats and look to him to continue.

"You are a teacher. Is that correct?" She nods. "Fourth grade?"

"Yes, I've taught a fourth grade class for the past three years. I taught second grade before that."

"School just ended for the year. What do you do during the summer?"

"Not a lot, really. I help my parents out with their

vegetable stand later in the summer, when their crops come in. I like to read, and I do a little writing."

"I see," is all Swann says. His smug look remains.

"The parents of your students don't mind that you have a criminal past?"

Ms. Davidson's eyes drop to her lap, but not before I can see the tears brewing.

"What exactly are you referring to?" Mr. Jamison asks impatiently.

"You know very well what I'm referring to since you were Ms. Davidson's counsel at the time. She was charged with drug possession."

"Those charges were dropped," her lawyer retorts. "When it was discovered that the *real criminal* was her husband. He was convicted and sent to prison for his crimes. Besides, you cannot be comparing marijuana possession with murder."

Yeah. I dig my nails into my palms to keep from cheering out loud. Whose side am I on here?

"All I'm saying is that maybe Ms. Davidson's husband had her involved in his drug business. Maybe she just didn't get caught."

Her lawyer stands. "Let's get this straight. Ms. Davidson's now *ex-husband* was involved in criminal activity. He went to prison, and she divorced him when she learned what he was involved in. She did not, in any way, willingly participate in his business, which is why her one measly charge was dropped. She is a law-abiding citizen. She was then, and she is now. Are you finished fishing? If so, we'd like to leave so that you can get busy finding the *real* criminal."

Swann doesn't seem at all phased by the tirade. He smiles. *Such an asshole.* I sneak a peek at Ms. Davidson. She's crying in earnest now. *Shit.*

Chapter Nine

Phoebe

"I just can't imagine what happened to your house key. We haven't used it since you locked yourself out last year. I know it was there a couple weeks ago, because I remember seeing the dragonfly keychain that it hangs on." Mom says again, probably for the eight hundredth time. I could really use a Twizzler right now.

Mom's grey eyes are filled with worry. Her petite five-foot-two-inch frame is a little hunched, showing the fatigue of the day. She usually has perfect posture, so it's noticeable when she's slumping. Lilly and I take after Dad's side of the family. I've had five inches over Mom since I was fifteen. My extra height never meant that I got away with anything. Mom's short stature just means that she throws a more powerful punch. Whether she's in Mom-temper-mode or Mom-love-mode, she gives it her all.

Dad is six-foot-one and still maintains a muscular physique. I guess working on a farm all your life will do that for you. He's still a very good-looking man. His hair has turned a distinguished grey, and he still has all of it, as far as I can tell. Dad's dark blue eyes and chiseled features are so nice that Mom has to get territorial sometimes with the occasional single lady her age. Some of them can come on pretty strong.

"You're sure you saw it there two weeks ago?" This is Dad's repeat follow-up. Then Mom says she's sure because she had to get Lilly's key when she helped babysit Hillary and Madison after school. Repeat. Repeat. Repeat. *I'm going to go insane.*

"It's okay." My turn in this script of insanity. Lilly was able to produce her copy of the key, but the one I keep with my parents is M.I.A. The detectives ended my interrogation and then drove to my parents' home to conduct theirs. *When did you last see the key? Could anyone else have taken it?* My parents haven't had any visitors in the last two weeks except Lilly's family and me. But, and this is a big but, my parents don't keep their own house locked much, so that brings up the possibility that my key could have been stolen from their kitchen. They keep all keys in their possession hanging on a key rack by the back door. Yes, it seems like a stretch, but if a key is the only way that someone could have gotten into my house last night, then someone had to have stolen it from my parents. There's no other way.

Luckily, Detective Swann doesn't seem to think my mom and dad are suspects. Mom said that both detectives were businesslike, very professional. It's bad enough that they act like I have something to hide. I don't know what I'd do if they started asking too much of my parents.

We are all having a big, not-so-fun family dinner at Lilly and Kevin's. After Mom tore apart her house looking for the missing key, she came over to Lilly's and began cooking a pork roast with mashed potatoes, green beans, and homemade rolls. Mom likes to cook when she's nervous.

John and his partner, Patrick, are here as well so that we can combine business with pleasure and discuss my case. *My case.* Why does it have to be mine? I don't want it.

John insists that the police have nothing concrete that ties me to the victim. Sure, he died in my house with one of my knives inside him, but all the evidence is circumstantial.

They've checked out my alibi, and they know that I was at Barney's between eight and ten o'clock. That information was from Barney himself. I spoke with him a few times while we were there, and he gave a vague description of my date, Jeffrey. They are still trying to contact Jeffrey. If he had come home with me last night, then at least I wouldn't have been alone when I found him. Can you imagine his relief at *not* going out with me again? He asked to come back to my place last night and then came on way too strong, so I blew him off. There was no chemistry there, not even enough for a second date.

There is plenty of chemistry between me and Detective Matthews, though. *Why him?* I feel shivers when he looks at me, not to mention when he touches me. I almost dropped the cup of water he was handing me at the police station. How embarrassing would that have been? Why can't I fall for someone accessible and not someone who is trying to put me in prison?

That isn't fair. Detective Swann is the one who has the attitude. Detective Matthews is helpful. *I think. Maybe.* He did come here this morning to make sure that I had a lawyer with me today.

But he was interrogating me in that room just like Detective Swann.

But that's his job.

Am I now arguing with myself?

"Phoebe?" I look up to see everyone's eyes upon me, giving me the hint that that wasn't the first time someone had said my name. The telltale blush creeps up my cheeks. Why do I have to look so guilty? They're going to know I was up to something.

"Yes?" I finally have to ask to break the silence.

"Mom was just saying that she'd like you to stay with her for a couple days."

Mom's grey eyes are full of worry. The same

anxious look is mirrored on my father's face. "I would just feel better with you at our house."

"It's definitely quieter there," Lilly adds. "Things are crazy here if the girls are home." That is true. Today after camp there were screams of joy when the girls were allowed to have friends over as long as they played outside and then screams of pain when Madison fell and skinned her knee on the driveway. Not quiet, but I like the activity of the girls running around, even with the occasional crying.

"I'll stay here, but just for one more night." Kevin's eyebrows raise. He looks like he can't believe that I'd stay here willingly. I defend myself and my nieces. "I like the noise."

"So one more night here, and then you'll come to our house?" Dad asks.

"No. Detective Swann said that my house is being released tomorrow. The crime scene cleaners I hired will clean it in the afternoon, and then I can go back home."

Mom gasps. "You want to go back there already?" The implied *Are you crazy?* that she didn't say out loud can't be missed.

"That is my home, and it's where I belong. My clothes are there. I don't want to borrow Lilly's clothes anymore. I just want to be home." Things aren't normal if I'm not home. If I'm going to get my life back together quickly, then that's where I need to be.

"I will change the locks tomorrow before you go

back," Kevin announces. Lilly gives him a traitorous glance. I give him a smile.

"Please reconsider," Mom practically begs.

"I want to be in my own house. That isn't crazy." They let it go, but I'm sure that this isn't the last that I'll hear of it.

Chapter Ten

Logan

"Turn around nice and slow there buddy."
What the hell?

I do as ordered. My eyes meet his, and I can see his determination, even in the dark. I can also see that he has a shotgun aimed directly at me, and he looks like he's not afraid to use it. How did I not hear him coming?

"What do you think you're doing?" he asks calmly.

He's not very tall, under six feet for sure, but he looks even shorter due to his slouched stature and bare feet. He doesn't have much hair, and what he has is stark white. His wrinkled face scrunches just before he spits to his right in a somehow graceful motion, as if he's been doing it his whole life—he probably has. I feel his stare pierce through me.

"I asked you a question."

"I was just checking on Ms. Davidson, um Phoebe. I didn't want to bother her, but I wanted to make sure that she's okay." Why do I suddenly feel like a pubescent teenager who's been caught by a protective father?

He sighs. "You know her?"

"Yes."

"We'll see about that?"

"Arnie, do I need to call the police?" A feminine, but gruff voice shouts from the yard of the house next door.

"Not yet, but keep the phone handy," he yells back.

Great. I can just imagine Fuller or one of the other guys answering that call. I would never live that down. I have to come clean.

"Actually, sir," I say as calmly as possible. "I'm the police." His eyes rove over me again from head to toe. "I have my badge in my left pocket."

"Okay, let's see it. Use one hand. Nice and easy." He motions toward my left side with the shotgun.

I fish in my pocket with my left hand and retrieve my badge. Arnie takes it from me and holds it up to catch the cast of his own porch light. He studies it closely and then lowers his gun. Relief courses through my veins, although I know that this is far from over.

"I'm Detective Matthews," I say as I sweep my

arm toward him.

"Arnie Huffman." His handshake is strong, and even though he's looking up at me, there is nothing small about this man.

"No need to call the police, Hon," he calls out. A door slams, and a woman walks toward us.

"This is my wife, Millie," he announces. She stops about twenty feet away and nods.

Phoebe's front door opens and then closes, and then she's with us as well. It's like a party out here. She's wearing plaid pajama pants and a tank top. She looks awake though, and I could tell that the television was on inside, so I don't think I woke her. Phoebe's eyes widen slightly when she sees me. Of course she's surprised.

"Do you know this guy?" Arnie asks Phoebe. "I caught him peeking in your windows. What has this world come to when the frickin' police are the peeping Toms?"

"It's not like that, sir," I say hastily and turn toward Phoebe. Her eyes are curious, but I detect a bit of amusement in them as well. She folds her arms over her chest. "I ran into your sister at the grocery store. She said that you were staying here tonight. I wanted to see if you were okay, but I didn't want to bother you."

"Ever heard of a telephone?" Arnie asks impatiently. He hocks another spit wad on Phoebe's lawn.

"I really didn't want to bother you." *And I didn't*

want a record of a phone call.

Phoebe smiles. It's a beautiful sight. "Thanks Arnie for protecting me, but I think I can take it from here." She walks to him and plants a kiss on his cheek. My own burns. *What the hell? Am I jealous of this old man?* "Goodnight, you two." Arnie and Millie continue to study me.

Phoebe turns without another word or glance in my direction and walks around to the front of the house. I follow her into her home, closing the door behind me. I really shouldn't be here. *So why can't I leave?*

She turns to me as we enter her house.

"Does Arnie know that it's illegal to hold someone at gunpoint? He found out I was a policeman, and he didn't even flinch."

"You aren't going to arrest him for that, are you?" she asks nervously. "He and Millie are very protective of me on a normal day, but with everything that happened…"

"I guess we can let this pass." Phoebe smiles, the relief evident on her face. She stands nearby, watching me. Some kind of current moves back and forth between us causing a disturbance in the air that I can feel.

"What are you doing here, and why are you peeping in my windows?" She finally asks.

What am I doing here? I don't know what to do, so I just stand here with my arms at my sides, staring at the floor. I feel her watching me as the awkward silence continues.

I lift my head and look into her eyes.

"What I said out there is true. Your sister is really upset that you're not still at her house or with your parents. She's worried about you. I thought I would just make sure that you're okay."

"Why can't you just call me or knock on the door like a normal person?"

"I'm not supposed to be talking to you." *Leave before this gets worse, you idiot.* "In fact, I'm going to go."

I turn toward the door, but she grips my forearm before I can reach the knob. Electricity flows between us where our skin touches. She turns me around, and I let myself face her. *Why am I doing this?* I need to run, flee, get out of here. But, I'm stuck. My feet are weighted and will not move from this spot.

Chapter Eleven

Phoebe

Add Detective Matthews to the list of the culprits spying on me. Who would have thought?

He looks so unsure. It just makes me like him even more.

I step closer—only about a foot away now. He doesn't move. I take another step until I'm inches from him, so close that I can smell his musky scent. I wish that I was dressed in something a little more alluring than my pajamas.

"Stay," I say. The word is barely a whisper.

His lips take mine. *Take* is the word that comes to mind because he claims them so completely. My mouth surrenders to him, and I'm on fire. There's nothing tentative about his tongue as it explores my mouth. His hands move to my shoulders and then my back as he pulls me tightly to him.

A moan echoes from deep inside me. I rake my hands through his dark hair. He pulls me even closer. The feel of his tight body brings sensations to places that have been dormant for way too long. One kiss, especially a first kiss, has never had this effect on me —from zero to sixty in five seconds flat.

He pulls back enough to break our kiss, but one hand still rests on my lower back, holding me close. His other hand caresses my cheek. His eyes hold an unmistakable fire that I'm sure is reflected in my own.

"I should apologize for that, but it wouldn't be sincere." The corners of my lips turn up to a smile that he returns. The hard lines of his face soften, the corners of his eyes wrinkle, and his eyes brighten. For a moment, all is right with the world. Until a hard punch of reality hits him, and his smile recedes. "Still, I shouldn't have kissed you. I can't believe that I came here."

He begins to pull away, but I refuse to let go. "I'm glad that you're here. Does that count for anything?"

He stills. His gaze drops to the floor. "I obviously have feelings for you, or I wouldn't have risked coming here in the first place. That doesn't change the fact that it's wrong. Until we charge someone with what happened, I should stay far away from you. This is highly inappropriate."

"Do you believe that I killed Ron Carpenter?"

His eyes meet mine. "No. Of course not."

"Good. Now, I was just going to sit down and watch a movie. Will you stay with me?" His shoulders slump in defeat. He nods. That isn't the enthusiastic answer that I was hoping for, but at least he's staying. I take his hand again and guide him to the couch. "Would you like a beer?"

"Sure," he answers quietly as he shifts uncomfortably on my couch. *Please don't bolt.*

"Be right back," I say with as much cheeriness as I can muster. It sounds fake to my own ears, but hopefully he won't notice. This is a good test for me —to walk into my kitchen. I tried earlier, but I couldn't do it. I stood in the dining room with tears sliding down my cheeks, wondering if I'm going to have to get take-out for the rest of the time that I live here. Even though the kitchen is spotless, and I see no evidence that he was ever actually here, the vision of *him* lying there is burned into my brain.

I don't want to move. I worked hard to get my life back together after my divorce and buy this house on my own. I don't want to do it again.

"Can I help?" a voice says behind me. I startle and turn to see him watching me. I realize that I'm standing again in the carpeted dining room, still unable to cross the line onto the kitchen linoleum. I'm unsure of how long I've been standing here.

"I really want to do it," I say softly. I feel stronger, having Detective Matthews behind me. *Detective Matthews.* "Can I call you Logan?" I ask sheepishly, feeling the blush creep up my neck.

"Definitely, at least when we're alone."

His words imply that there may be other times that we're alone. I like it. He smiles, and it gives me the courage to take the first step. I suppress a shudder as I move toward the refrigerator. I make my movements quick, but I'm successful at grabbing the beers and making it back to the safety of the carpeted dining room. Relief washes over me at the hope that the next time will be better and then better and better after that.

I can do this.

Logan wraps a strong arm around my shoulders and presses a kiss onto my forehead. He smiles down at me and walks me back to the living room. We sit together on the couch, close enough that our thighs brush, radiating awareness to my most private of areas.

I feel his eyes on me, but I stay focused on the television. I need a moment to process this. There is a man in my house. I've gone a long time without seriously dating anyone, and now I have a hot police detective sitting with me while I'm in my PJs. This is so not normal for me. *And that kiss.* That was the most incredible kiss of my life. I still feel the pulses of current flowing through me. *Incredible.* I sneak a look in his direction.

"So, why Hickory Grove?"

He takes a pull of his beer. "I needed a change, and Hickory Grove needed a detective." Another short answer. Moving on.

"Do you have family in Miami?"

"No." *Really?*

"Do you have family anywhere?"

"My dad and step-mother are in a senior citizen community outside of Jacksonville. We aren't close. I have a younger brother in the army, stationed in Germany. We are closer, but I don't get to see him much." I smile, and it turns into a small chuckle. "Is that funny?"

I smile more and shake my head. I tend to get a little giddy when I'm this exhausted. "No. It's just that you finally gave me a real answer. You're not much of a talker."

"I'm just preoccupied. Why did you come back here so soon?"

I turn my body toward him so that I can see his face—full of concern. I place my beer on the coffee table and watch my hands as they clasp together in my lap.

"I told you. This is my home. It's where I belong."

"You don't have to be strong you know. You've been through a lot, and you should allow yourself the time you need to get over this."

I shrug my shoulders. "I just want my life back to normal. I wasted too much of it in a daze when I discovered the truth about my ex-husband, Alan. It was devastating to find out that someone I loved could hide so much from me. I was a mess, and I refuse to go through another experience like that. I want this nightmare over as soon as possible."

He covers my hands with his and squeezes.

Chapter Twelve

Logan

I am in so much trouble. I was attracted to Phoebe before, but the determined look in her eyes makes me feel something new, something that I can't or don't want to identify. All I know for sure is that being here with her is right. Maybe it isn't the right thing to do for my job, but in a higher way, this is where I belong.

This doesn't even make sense. I left Miami because of the corruption, and here I am pulling the same kind of crap that I was so against there.

This is different.

But is it really?

Yes? This kind of thing happens on a regular basis in my old precinct and is one of the reasons I left. I can't believe that I'm here now, but there's no way that I'm leaving either.

I lean toward her and press my lips gently against her cheek.

"Phoebe." I wanted to see how it would feel to say her name. The word comes out as a whisper, and my body responds. I lean toward her for a kiss, but she's already here, kissing me instead. Fire shoots through me as soon as her lips meet mine. She slips her hands under my t-shirt, tugging it upwards. The heat of her fingers on my bare skin takes my breath away. I literally have to concentrate to breathe. We break our kiss as she lifts my shirt over my head.

Phoebe's shirt comes next, revealing her full breasts through a sheer ivory bra. "Beautiful," I murmur as I kiss her through the lace. Soon even that becomes too much of an impediment, and I remove her bra altogether. She gasps and begins working on the button of my jeans.

Are we really going to do this?

I don't think I've ever needed anything more, but I have to know that this is what she wants, too.

"Are you sure?" I ask softly, feeling like part of me will die if she stops us. Her eyes meet mine, all soft and full. I wait in agony for her answer as she catches her breath.

"Please...*don't stop*." Her cheeks flush as she speaks. She averts her eyes suddenly. Is she embarrassed? She can't be. She was just trying to unbutton my jeans. The thought makes me like her even more. I stand and swoop her up with me. If we're going through with this, we can at least be in her bed. Her arms slip around my neck as I carry her down the hallway to her bedroom. She plants tiny kisses on my chest on the way.

I lay her down carefully on the bed and slowly slide off her pants, leaving her clothed in nothing more than a scrap of lace. Need surges through me as I take in her flushed body before me. *Amazing.* I quickly slide down my jeans and boxers and lie down beside her. I keep worrying that she will change her mind, that this won't happen, but the way that she moves against me tells me otherwise.

My fingers move beneath her panties. She reaches down and removes them herself, leaving us both naked.

"Logan." Her husky whisper of my name is more than I can stand. I cover her body and make her mine.

Chapter Thirteen

Phoebe

I can't believe that we just did that.

No, I believe we did, and I'm glad. It was absolutely incredible.

I just can't believe that I instigated it. That wasn't me. *Me.* This isn't something I do. I don't have sex with men that I barely know. I don't have sex with anybody. Geez. Based on my track record, I only have sex with men who are, or will end up to be, my husband. More surprising than the fact that I did just now totally have sex with a hot detective, is that I don't feel remorseful about it in the least. Logan even gave me an out, and I didn't take it. He must think I'm some kind of slut. Can you be a slut at thirty-one, or is that a term reserved for younger women?

I know that I like him—a lot. Was it the need for Logan or the need for *someone?* Six years is a long time to go without sex.

Six years.

I've had opportunities during that time when I could have jumped the person I was with, like I just jumped Logan, and they would have gone along with it. Guys are much more easygoing about such things, right? I didn't want anyone else. I can't just have sex to have sex; there needs to be some real feeling behind it.

There was this one guy that I dated for a while. I didn't swoon around him, but he was a nice guy, so I really tried to give it my all. We'd been together for just over a month, and I decided that maybe I just needed a push. We would finally have sex—he'd been trying since the second date—and maybe then I would fall hopelessly in love, and that would be that. When the time came, I couldn't go through with it. I felt so sick to my stomach that I had to run to the bathroom for fear of throwing up. That was kind of a mood-killer. I thought it was just nerves since I had only ever been with Alan, but as I lay there on the cool, tile floor, I knew that it was just wrong. I let it continue much too far and then couldn't go through with it. He left in a huff, and I don't blame him at all. Fortunately, he was from a couple towns away, and I've never run into him again.

I've analyzed the situation a bazillion times. I have trust issues. How could I not? I knew Alan for years before we married, and if I didn't really know him, then how can I really know anyone? But, here I am with someone I barely know at all, and I trusted him immediately. So it isn't just anyone, it's Logan.

I sneak a look at him as he lies next to me. His chest rises and falls rapidly as he tries to catch his breath. A new batch of lust flows through me as I take in his muscular chest and remember how he felt moving against me. His eyes meet mine, and I look away. Heat sears my cheeks again. I just hope I'm so flushed already from our love fest that he can't tell I'm blushing.

What he must think of me.

Men and women do this all the time. I shouldn't be worrying so much about it. Just because I have never had sex with someone that I've only known a few days, doesn't mean that other people don't do it all the time. Maybe this is totally normal for him.

One look at Logan, and I know that isn't true. His eyes are concerned, no longer dark with the fire of making love. I feel the heat of his gaze as he studies me. I don't know what to say.

"Do you regret this already? You don't even need more time to think about it before you wish you hadn't done it?" I can't miss the hurt in his tone.

"No," I bite back quickly. "I'm glad...that it happened." His brow furrows in confusion. "I'm...I'm just embarrassed because I practically jumped you, and now I don't know how to act. I don't know what you think of me. I barely know you. This...this isn't me." My eyes are wet now. *Great.*

Logan's hand finds my shoulder and squeezes. "Would it help if I tell you something about me? Maybe something that I've never told anyone else?"

Interesting. I feel the corners of my mouth tip up into a smile. "Sure."

"Okay. Let me think." His fingertips lazily brush my shoulder, warming it with his touch. I didn't even know my shoulder could feel tingly. Logan sighs heavily. His smile covers his entire face. "You have to promise that you will never tell a soul."

"Scouts honor." The left corner of Logan's mouth curves to a smirk.

"When I was a kid, I peed outdoors until I was nine."

I chuckle. "Why?"

"I just didn't like bathrooms." His eyes dart away from mine.

"Is that the real reason?" He shrugs. There's another reason, but he doesn't want to share it. "What about your *other* bathroom business?"

"I took care of *that* where I was supposed to. I pitched such a fit about it that my mom and I made a deal. If I did *that* where I was supposed to, then I could wash my hair and body in the kitchen and pee behind the garage. Our agreement ended when I was nine. One afternoon I got in a hurry and didn't go in a *hidden* area. Maggie Donohue, the girl next door, saw me pee in the back yard, and that was the end of that."

I can feel that I'm a little wide-eyed after his story. "I can trust that you're house-trained now, right?"

Logan nods. "Okay. Your turn. Scouts honor that I won't tell anyone either."

"Not yet. You see, you said it had to be something that no one knows about you, but you told me something that at least your mother and Maggie Donohue know. So, technically, that doesn't meet the requirements you laid out. You're going to have to tell me something else."

"You drive a hard bargain, but you have to give me something first, and it has to be *good*. How do I know that you aren't gathering all my secrets to sell to the tabloids?"

"If their offer is good enough, I might just do that." His eyes flicker with a hint of surprise, and then he laughs a deep laugh. I feel it vibrate through my hot zones. "I like hot sauce on waffles."

His head shakes slowly from side to side. "You can do better than that."

I search my brain for something to say. I want it to be real, but I don't want it to scare the crap out of him. "In the eleventh grade, Devon Patterson had a big party, and I went with some friends. It was my first *real* party. There was a group of girls there who didn't like me very much. I will spare you the teenage girl drama. Just suffice it to say that they were spiteful. One of them, Trisha Marconi, told me that I was fat." Logan's eyes widen slightly. "Yeah, I know. So, when she went to the bathroom and no one was looking, I spit in her beer." His deep laugh rumbles, shaking the mattress, and me, too. "I watched her drink it for the next half hour, and I couldn't get the smile off of my face."

"Nice. What else?"

"No way. Your turn."

"All right. I like odd numbers."

"What does that mean?"

"Everyone I've ever known seems to favor even numbers when asked—favorite number, or choose a number, or whatever. My cousin can't even have the television volume on an odd number, even if it's too loud or too soft on an even one." I tilt my head slightly, not buying that this is a *thing*. "What's your favorite number?"

"Seven."

His mouth curves into a luscious smile. "I guess there are some exceptions. Your turn."

"I like Disney cartoons." Crap. It just blurted out before it was properly vetted.

Logan immediately begins shaking his head. "That's not a secret. Everyone likes Disney cartoons."

"*The Little Mermaid* is my favorite, and I've watched it more times than I can count." His head tilts toward the mattress. "No, really. I've watched it more than a hundred times, probably way more."

"And no one knows about this mermaid obsession?"

"No. My family knows that I like it, but I watch it

when no one's around." *Of course, that isn't something that's difficult to do since Alan and I split.* Logan leans up on his elbow. The prickles of heat travel from my neck to my face at the speed of light; the sudden warmth, combined with the emotion of the last few days, makes me light-headed. I focus on a wrinkle in the sheet between us. I can't look at him. "I knew I shouldn't have told you that. You probably want to leave now." *And you probably should leave before I start crying uncontrollably.*

Logan's fingers cup my chin, and he tilts it upward. My eyes resist at first but finally give in. He smiles, and at this moment, it's the most beautiful sight I've ever seen. "You know that there is something here, right? You feel it, too?"

"Yes." The word comes out as a throaty whisper.

"What I think is that you are the answer to my prayers, and that we should do that at least two more times."

Relief washes over me, leaving me dizzy yet again. Logan wraps a protective arm around me and pulls me to him.

***

A gentle pressure against my cheek awakens me. Logan stands over me in my darkened bedroom. He kneels down next to the bed and takes my hand in his.

"I have to go," he says quietly. "I was thinking that

maybe I will officially remove myself from your case. Then I won't have to sneak around your house to visit, and I can call you to ask you out on an official date. What do you think?"

I smile. "I would like that."

"Good because I like you too much for this to be a secret. I'll see you soon. Okay?"

"Yeah." After another kiss on the cheek he's gone.

I stretch and move my hand to Logan's side of the bed. It's still a little warm. I hug his pillow to me and smile as visions of our night together flow through my mind. Any embarrassment I had is long gone. I'm left feeling elated. He likes me. I like him. Maybe this isn't the way I normally do things, but I'm happy. Plus, I had no nightmares about the dead man in my house. I slept soundly and peacefully.

I take a long shower and busy myself with household stuff. I pay my bills and do some laundry, and I do it all without coffee because despite my bravery last night, I'm still afraid to go into the kitchen. I don't even want to look at it. So I keep to the living room, my bedroom, and office.

By nine o'clock I realize that I can't do without caffeine, so a trip to our little coffee shop is in order. I generally find it best to avoid this place. They have good food and great coffee, but they also have Joy Rogers, and she's not so great. It's a long story, but she's the ex-girlfriend of my ex-husband. That sounds so soap opera. It's been years since it should even matter, but I've become practiced at avoiding

Joy, and I guess some habits are hard to break.

She is not at the cash register when I enter the building, so I take that as an omen that this is going to be a great day. I get a large dark roast coffee along with a breakfast sandwich to go. I return home, singing along with the pop songs that play on the car radio. I feel happier than I have in ages, and I know that it's all because of Logan. I have zero regrets about our night together, and I'm excited to spend more time with him and get to know him better. This is something special. I can feel it. I'm not in a hurry to jump into a super-serious relationship—too many battle scars for that—but I'm willing to take it super slow to see where it goes. Kind of a funny thought since the physical part of our relationship has moved at lightning speed.

My happy thoughts are put on hold when I see the action at my home. Two police cruisers and an unmarked car that is obviously still a police vehicle are parked on the street in front of my little house. My legs feel like jelly as I climb out of my car. Detective Swann saunters across my yard toward me.

"We have a search warrant for your residence. Will you cooperate and unlock your door?"

I nod and take some uneven steps toward my house. I hold my head high—I have nothing to hide —but Mrs. Miller is watching the scene from across the street. I open the door for Detective Swann and watch in silence as he and four uniformed policemen enter my home.

I need to call John.

I stumble back to my car where Logan intercepts me. "I'm sorry that this is happening," he whispers in hushed tones. His chocolate eyes are cloudy, like they are forecasting the storminess of the situation. "I didn't know about it. I swear. Swann was ready to go with this as soon as I got to the station."

"I thought you were going to remove yourself from this investigation." I throw down the challenge. That's what he said just a couple hours ago when he left my bed. *My bed*. Now he's here, violating my privacy.

"I can't do that. Not now."

"Leave me alone."

"Phoebe, please."

"That's *Ms. Davidson* to you."

"It's not like..." Logan doesn't get to finish his sentence. Arnie interrupts.

"I believe she asked you to leave her alone. Now why don't you go about your business and do just that?"

Our eyes turn to Arnie. He's wearing his usual baggy jeans and a faded green t-shirt with a big fish on the front. His hands are placed on his hips. His shoulders are set, his lips pressed into a hard line. He holds no gun and yet, somehow doesn't need one to be intimidating.

Logan takes a step back. His face is drawn and sorrowful. What he's sorry for, I don't know. Is he sorry that he's on my doorstep with a search warrant just after he left it? Is he sorry that he saw something when he was here last night that required a closer look, so he decided my house needed to be searched? He told me that he was going to be removed from my case so that we could be together, and here he is with *them,* invading my property. It's not right.

Arnie's thin but muscular arm slides around my shoulders. He stands with me as I watch Logan turn and walk into my house. I'm more concerned with Logan's betrayal than with the fact that the police are searching my house. I know that I didn't do anything wrong. I have nothing to hide. That helps with the police side of things, but nothing helps with Logan. At least with Alan, it was a gradual demise. That's not the case this time.

"Come on over and wait at our house," Arnie says softly.

I reach inside my Civic and grab my coffee, breakfast, and purse. I won't be needing breakfast anymore. I need to call my lawyer.

Chapter Fourteen

Logan

The betrayal was all over her face. Of course it was. From her side of things, I look like a complete shit. When I told her *see you later*, I didn't think that it would be like this. Swann got some kind of tip that Phoebe is lying about knowing the victim. Phoebe says she doesn't know him. I believe her. Hopefully the *tip* came from some crackpot, and we can get through this search without finding anything. Once Swann sees there's nothing here, then we can move on to look for the real murderer.

I can't quit this case now. I'm not trying to give her any special treatment—*I will not give her special treatment*—but I need to be here to temper Swann's insistence that Phoebe's involved in this crime. Any level-headed person would see that she's a victim and nothing more. There isn't one bit of evidence so far that shows Phoebe is involved in this. The sooner Swann understands that, the sooner we can get on with finding the real criminal.

My heart slams into my chest when I see the couch. I close my eyes and steady myself against the onslaught of visions from our night together. The way her full breasts looked as they bulged from the top of her lace bra. The flush of her body as she watched me discard my jeans. The feel of her beside me and then me inside her. I don't regret one moment of being with Phoebe. I only regret being here now as an outsider. I regret not being able to make this all go away.

Why am I having these thoughts? Why am I in this situation at all? I've been accused of being the *goody-goody* cop. The guys on the force in Miami would freak if they found out about my current predicament. *Mr. Rule-Follower* breaking the rules. My old partner, Paul, would never believe it.

I watch as Mason searches through Phoebe's DVDs. Fuller carries her laptop out the front door. Let them look. They aren't going to find anything. That's what I think, but my gut tells me that this is far from over.

A slight panic hits me. I force myself to walk and not run to Phoebe's bedroom. I'm in trouble enough with Phoebe. I don't need them to find male DNA, *my DNA*, all over the sheets.

Her bed is made.

"You take the bedroom," Swann tells me as he walks up behind me. I nod acceptance, but fuck, what am I going to do if I find something?

I grab a kit from the living room and begin with the bed. I will check the whole room, but I have to see what's here first. I run the black light over the exposed sheets. Nothing. Relief washes through me at the sight of her clean sheets.

She changed the sheets.

One more thing to check before celebrating. I walk back into the hallway and slide open the door to the small laundry room. It's more of a closet really. The washer and dryer sit silently. I open the door of the washer to find a load of wet clothes.

Please.

I find just what I want to see in the dryer, a set of dry and very *clean* sheets.

Thank you, God.

Thank you, Phoebe.

My knees weaken, and I lean on the door jamb as the relief takes me. Sure I'm relieved that I still have my job, but I'm also relieved for Phoebe. Having a man in her life would definitely complicate the investigation, and neither of us need that.

***

Our search yields only one thing of interest—my shoe prints. Officer Mason found the indentions my shoes made in the flower bed when I leaned in to look into Phoebe's window last night. He made a cast of them. Fortunately, the shoes I was wearing have completely flat bottoms, nothing remarkable or identifiable. Also in the plus column, I did not lean in onto the window and leave any fingerprints or DNA behind. If I had, I would be screwed.

Swann isn't sure what to make of the footprints. He declares that they could be from a nosy neighbor or totally unrelated. He knows that they were not here when we searched the house and property the night of the murder, so he feels they're probably inconsequential to the case. Besides, in Swann's mind, if it doesn't help prove Phoebe's guilt, then he will likely ignore it.

Phoebe's laptop will be looked over at the lab. It will be clean, and this will be over.

I accompany Swann next-door to inform Phoebe that we're finished. Swann wants to ask a few questions of the neighbors. I pray that Arnie and his wife won't rat me out for visiting Phoebe last night. Do they know that Phoebe and I are on the down low? It shouldn't be hard to figure out considering the sneaking around I was doing last night.

Arnie answers the door. His stare bores a hole through Swann and me both. We introduce ourselves to Arnie and then to Millie as she joins us. Both act like they're meeting me for the first time. Swann seems more amused by Arnie than anything else. Arnie does not invite us inside.

Chapter Fifteen

Phoebe

"Phoebe, the detectives are here to see you," Arnie shouts from the front of the house. Their arrival is not a surprise. We saw them walking this way. We've been sitting at Arnie and Millie's kitchen table, watching the policemen coming and going from my house.

Millie has fussed over me the whole time I've been here trying to get me to eat, but I have no appetite with all of this going on. I barely even touched my coffee—the same coffee that only two hours ago I thought was important enough to make a special trip for and risk seeing Joy Rogers. I don't think I could get a Twizzler down at this point, and it's bad if I can't eat a Twizzler.

Arnie and Millie are about the best neighbors

that a girl could ask for. They are kind and generous, and they've adopted me as practically part of their family. Arnie tries to play the tough guy. Actually, there is no *playing* about it. *He is a tough guy*. But he's a tough guy with a softer side. So, if the world ends and we need to live by our wits alone to survive, then I'm going with Arnie. But he's the same guy who uses his snow thrower to clear my driveway when I need it, and Mrs. Miller's too. He's kind of like my foster grandfather, which is nice since my own passed away when I was twelve.

I rise and do my best to stand tall. I'm a strong woman. I have nothing to be ashamed of and nothing to hide. I will not cower before them, especially Logan. I walk into the front room, making sure to keep eye contact with both of them along the way. Detective Swann's expression is flat. He doesn't look thrilled, but he doesn't look evil either.

It's harder to look at Logan, but I do make the switch. His eyes are bright, intently meeting mine. A flash of how he looked at me last night sparks in my mind. His eyes were darker then, full of need for me. Now they're full of anxiety. Maybe he's afraid I will tell Swann. Shoot, maybe Swann put Logan up to last night to get more information. No, I don't really believe that's true, and either way, I'm not going there. I was not tricked into sleeping with Logan—I went willingly down that road. I may not be the kind of person who would normally jump into bed with a practical stranger, but I'm definitely not the kind of person to sell out someone that I love.

Love? Did I just think that? I feel the telltale prickles of my blush beginning to creep up my neck. *Love* might be a bit of a stretch, but what I feel for Logan is something more than *like*. It could be that I'm only allowing myself to think that to justify the fact that I slept with him. There's no way I'm in love with him or letting him into my life in that way. I've been burned enough—not going through that again.

Regardless of how I feel about Logan, I'm not going to tell anyone about him. I don't, however, mind watching him squirm for a bit. Let him worry that I, or maybe Arnie or Millie, will tell Detective Swann about what happened between us. They promised not to say anything, but Logan doesn't know that.

"Detective Matthews. Detective Swann," I say with a nod of greeting as I reach them. "May I return to my home now?" A little formal for me, but I feel like formality is called for in this situation.

Logan looks down at the floor. Detective Swann answers, "You are free to go. We have your laptop in our custody and will return it to you as soon as we are finished with it."

I say a curt *thank you*, grab my purse off a nearby chair, and hug Arnie and Millie goodbye. I would expect the detectives to depart, but they don't, so I walk back over to my house alone. I get the creepy feeling that comes with being watched, but this time the culprit is obvious. I wave to Mrs. Miller who's sitting on the porch of her house across the street. Apparently I'm her entertainment for the day. She's a sweet lady, even if a little on the nosey side.

Our neighborhood is made up of identical cozy, three-bedroom homes. There may have been a garage or carport added at some point, and the paint is different, but they're all pretty much the same. The houses are tiny, and the lots where the houses sit are almost as small, which makes them perfect for families just starting out and those who have raised their children and are looking for an affordable place to live out their senior years.

I steel myself as I open the front door, not sure what to expect. I walk through the rooms but find very little out of place. If the police were thorough with their searching, and I'm sure they were, then at least they were neat about it.

I call John and tell him that the police are finished with their search. "What happens now?" I ask.

"Now, we wait. Hopefully, this will be the end of the trail with you, and they can move on to finding the real criminal. I will contact you as soon as I hear something."

We say our goodbyes, and I'm left with a hollow feeling. What am I supposed to do now?

The answer comes with the ringing of the doorbell. It's Millie. Her bright smile greets me as I open the door. Millie has worked her fingers to the bone raising four boys and working in a local furniture factory for most of her life, but somehow all those wrinkles translate to the most peaceful face. She grabs my hands in hers and then pulls me out onto my little porch for a tight hug.

"You poor dear," she says softly. I let myself be wrapped in her softness, but the sweet moment is spoiled as my arms prickle with goose bumps. I'm being watched again. *Again.* I look up and down the street and see no one who's obviously staring. Mrs. Miller has gone inside, but maybe she's watching me out the window. The unmarked car is still parked on the street. Maybe Logan is still around somewhere, and he's the culprit. Regardless, it's nerve-racking and the last thing that I need today. My sanity is on the brink as it is. I pull Millie back inside the house with me.

"Those detectives asked us all kinds of questions about you," she says as we're settled at my small dining room table. I take a seat facing the living room, so I don't have to view the kitchen. Millie is staring at the kitchen, but in her eyes it probably doesn't look any different than it always has. She didn't see the dead man there.

I sigh heavily. "What did they want to know?"

"All kinds of things. We didn't tell them anything bad. We have nothing bad to tell. You're a good girl." She pats my hand softly. "They asked a few questions about your habits. They asked about your friends and if you were dating anyone." I feel my eyes widen a little. "Oh, don't worry. We didn't say anything about your detective friend, but boy was he fidgeting like he had ants in his pants." A huge smile takes over Millie's face, and before we know it, we're both laughing.

It feels so good to laugh.

Chapter Sixteen

Logan

Phoebe is a wonderful person and neighbor.

That's the glowing recommendation given to us by every person that we spoke with today. She's a great teacher. Her students love her, but she isn't a pushover. She helps her elderly neighbors with chores around the house when needed. It sounds like she's a saint. That is *not* what Swann wanted to hear. He became more downtrodden with each visit.

I thought I was done for when we spoke with Arnie and Millie. Arnie didn't lie, but he didn't mention that he found me hiding in Phoebe's bushes either. His eyes were brutal though as he explained that he hasn't known Phoebe to seriously date anyone since her divorce. I felt more threatened with this conversation than when he held me at gunpoint. It's at least just as bad. I could literally lose my life, or I could lose my job, not much difference in my book.

I found myself almost cheering on the inside every time Phoebe was praised. I have lost all objectivity. Hopefully this waste of a day will end Swann's obsession with Phoebe, and we can move on. The trail of the real killer is getting cold.

We head back to the station around three. I busy myself with paperwork. Swann's practically pacing as he waits for Jacobson, the lab guy, to finish going through Phoebe's computer. It's his last hope. I know they won't find anything there, but I'm still not going to let myself relax, not until the fat lady has sung the finale.

I finally leave at six with the promise to keep my phone handy. Jacobson plans to work late to go through Phoebe's computer. He's the only tech guy we have on staff, and he works a ton, even in this town. But this is a huge case and a top priority.

Back in Miami, I spent a lot of time with my partner. Paul is a little older than me and has a family. I practically ate more meals with them than I did alone. There was a bond there that made it work. We relied on each other. We were exponentially stronger as a team than as individuals, and I would still be there working with him if he hadn't gotten hurt.

That isn't the case here. Swann packs up and practically runs out the door each night. There's no invitation to come over for dinner. I think he's actually trying to get out of here before I ask him if he's going for a beer at Barney's. I know a few of the guys go there each day after work to blow off steam and, lately, commiserate that I got this job instead of Mason. How is this partnership ever going to work?

***

I go with the not-so-straightforward approach of knocking on Phoebe's back door this time. No peeking through the windows, but I'm not bold enough to go to her front door either. When the door opens, I can see immediately that she's pissed. Her forehead is scrunched, and her lips are set in a firm line.

"What do you want?"

"I just want to talk to you," I answer softly.

She stands her ground, one hand on her hip, and the other on the door, ready to slam it in my face. I watch as she chews on her lower lip as if deciding if she's going to let me in or not.

I expected to find her in pajamas or sweatpants or something of the sort. Instead, she's wearing a tank top sweater and a flowing skirt that stops just above her knee. Her feet are bare. She looks beautiful, and I'm at half-mast just from the sight of her.

"I want to explain." I bring my hand around to show her the special bouquet I've made for her—

Twizzlers tied in a bundle with a white ribbon. They flare at the top like flowers. "This is my peace offering."

Phoebe sighs and moves out of the way for me to enter. She takes the *bouquet* from me and places it carefully on the table. Her arms fold across her chest.

"Okay, let's hear it."

I glance toward the living room. She hasn't invited me to have a seat on the couch or even at the table. She stands in front of me, waiting for me to begin. Feelings crash over me in waves. I want to pull her to me and kiss the living daylights out of her, to let her know that I need her. I don't do that. I keep my arms at my sides.

"I had every intention of removing myself from your case, just like I said I would. But when I got to the station, Swann was ready to go with the search warrant. He wants to be thoroughly sure that you're not involved with the murder." She exhales quickly, a heavy, breathy sound. "I have more reason than ever to quit, but I can't. Swann is out to nail you, and I'm not going to let him do that. I have a much better chance of proving your innocence if I'm still working with him on the case."

"He will figure it out on his own anyway, whether you are there or not. I am innocent, so there's nothing he's going to find to prove otherwise. Do you know what kind of a slap in the face it was to see you here with them this morning, violating my home?"

I nod carefully. I think that was more of a rhetorical question, but it was awful. "I'm sorry." A lone tear falls down her cheek, her beautiful blue eyes are wet, threatening to release more. I take a step toward her and brush my thumb against her soft skin to wipe it way. "I know you're innocent, but I have to do my job. Let me help you prove it."

Chapter Seventeen

Phoebe

I want to be mad at Logan, and I want to hold my ground, but I want him to hold me more. I step into him, and his strong arms move around me in a cocoon of warmth. He rubs his hands up and down my back in soothing movements. I lay my head on his shoulder and melt into him. His heat spreads through my entire body.

When the warmth turns to a tingling, I lift my head to look at him. His eyes have darkened, but he doesn't make a move. He's waiting for me. I bring my lips to his—just a graze—but I feel it in my toes. I nibble his bottom lip. Logan moans. My mouth takes his, and our tongues move together, exploring, tasting. My hands move behind his neck, and I pull him closer to me. I need him closer.

His hands are on my hips, brushing me against him. My fingers move to the button of his dress slacks. They're unbuttoned, unzipped, and pushed down his thighs in no time. I wrap my hand around him and squeeze. A ragged sound escapes as he whispers my name. A need like I've never felt shoots through me.

Logan moves his hands to my butt and lifts me up. My legs move around him as he steadies me against the wall behind me. He lifts my skirt, slides my panties to the side, and thrusts into me. A shiver of ecstasy rips through my body and then again and again until we fall to the floor, spent and unable to stand.

Heaven.

We lie together smiling, staring into each other's eyes, after sharing what has to be the most insanely wonderful sexual experience of my life. I've never done anything remotely that exciting or hot, and I have never felt like this. I can't wipe the smile off my face as I wonder again what has happened to me. Prim and proper Phoebe has turned into a sex fiend.

The quiet of the house is shattered by the ringing of Logan's phone. With an apologetic smile, he reaches into his pants pocket and brings the phone to his ear.

"Matthews," he answers curtly. He listens as I watch the happiness drain from his eyes and then his face. He sits up straight, never taking his eyes off me. "Are you sure?" Dread washes over me. *This is bad.* "Got it. Be there in ten." He disconnects the call.

"Fuck!" Logan shouts. "You said that you didn't know him." The anger is coming off of him now in waves. The happiness from thirty seconds ago has evaporated.

"Who? Ron Carpenter?" I ask. Logan stands and begins pulling up his pants. I sit up and make it to my knees before I realize I'm too dizzy from our lovemaking to stand. "What are you talking about?"

"Yes. Ron Carpenter. You said that you didn't know him, and I believed you. I thought Swann was an idiot for not trusting you. I guess I'm the idiot.

"I didn't know him. I don't know him." I fight back. "What's going on?"

"Still playing the innocent game? Well, I guess that will end soon enough," he counters as he walks out the back door without so much as another look in my direction.

I fall back to the floor and try to wrap my head around this. One minute I'm sharing the most wonderfully intimate moment with Logan that I've ever had, and the next, he's yelling at me, his voice dripping with betrayal. Could Swann have found something linking me to Ron Carpenter?

But I don't know Ron Carpenter.

Yet, whatever they found must be pretty damning if Logan believes it so readily. I swallow the lump in my throat and head to the bathroom for a shower. I have a feeling that this is going to be a very long and very painful night.

Chapter Eighteen

Logan

Insanity.

This is complete insanity.

I believed everything that Phoebe told me. I bought every single thing she said. And then I fell head over heels for her. Was this all part of her back-up plan, in case she didn't get away with it on her own? It's like the icing on the cake.

Being with Phoebe was the most incredible sex I've ever had, but it wasn't just hot sex. There were feelings behind it. I thought that they went both ways. I've been with plenty of women. They've thrown themselves at me for my entire adult life, and not one of them has ever stirred up these feelings in me like this woman has.

I thought I was smarter than this—smart enough

not to get involved in this kind of thing. Will she blackmail me now? Get her out of this, or she'll expose my unethical behavior? Was that her plan all along? Seduce the stupid cop, so I would have to help her out?

But I can't believe she's capable of murder. She just can't be. And I don't think it's my *other head* hoping she's innocent. She is...and I fucking freaked on her. I didn't even give her a chance to explain. I just left, probably blowing any chance of a future together.

Swann is smiling from ear to ear. These emails are exactly the kind of thing he's been looking for to make our case. I have no idea how to explain them away, but there has to be a way. Phoebe is innocent.

"I called John Jamison and told him to get over here with his client. I don't care if it's late. I want some answers." I nod and excuse myself to get some coffee. I wish I had something stronger.

***

Phoebe, her lawyer, and her parents descend upon us forty-five minutes later. Phoebe is dressed in a skirt, a different one *thank God*, but I still feel the prickles of heat on my neck at the memory of what we were doing only an hour ago. I try to make eye contact with her, but she won't look directly at me. I want her to know that I'm sorry for running out on her. Can't blame her though. She deserves better than that.

Her facial expression is set on dumbfounded. Please let it be that she's really innocent and not just a really good actress.

We settle into the interrogation room and take the same seats that we had the other day. Phoebe and her lawyer are here with us. Her parents have to wait outside. They seem like nice enough people. Phoebe's mother fusses over her, dutifully outraged at the mere thought that her sweet daughter could have done anything illegal. The evidence seems pretty iron clad. I'm hoping for a reasonable explanation, but someone needs to tell them to stop kidding themselves and prepare for the worst, just in case.

Phoebe and her lawyer decline our offer of coffee, and now that the pleasantries are over, Swann gets down to business.

"As you know Ms. Davidson, we confiscated your laptop this morning as part of our search of your home."

She nods. "Yes, I'm aware of that."

"Does anyone else have access to your computer?"

"No. Just me."

"Are you sure?"

Phoebe sighs. "Yes, I'm sure. It rarely even leaves my house."

"And you live alone?"

"Yes," she answers almost as a growl.

"Ms. Davidson, you have told us on several occasions that you *did not* know the deceased, Mr. Ron Carpenter."

Phoebe sighs. "That is correct. I. Did. Not. Know. Mr. Carpenter. I don't recall ever seeing him before I found him on my kitchen floor." Swann smirks.

Her jaw and shoulders are rigid as she waits for the ball to drop.

"Aren't you clever there, Ms. Davidson? You just said that you never *saw* him before, but you neglected to mention that you had been corresponding with Mr. Carpenter in emails for over a week."

Phoebe's jaw drops. Her eyes widen. "That is ridiculous. I did no such thing." Her chest rises and falls quickly, each breath a gasp of air. I will her to look at me, but she focuses on Swann. If she would look at me, maybe she could tell that I'm on her side. I believe her.

"Yet we have the emails here to prove it. They were found on your computer in your deleted mail folder. You're a smart woman, Ms. Davidson. You'd think you'd be smart enough to know that nothing is truly deleted."

"That's impossible," she repeats, this time as a whisper. She slumps a little lower in her chair.

"Let me see those," her lawyer counters.

Swann slides a short stack of papers over to Mr. Jamison and continues. "You *flirted with* and *propositioned* Mr. Carpenter via email until he agreed to meet with you to discuss a business venture."

"What kind of business venture?" Phoebe asks, surprise in her eyes.

"You can cut the innocent act, Ms. Davidson. We have the proof."

Chapter Nineteen

Phoebe

The words echo in my mind, reminding me of Logan's similar statement just before he ran away from me earlier this evening. The memory of Logan's harsh tone shakes my insides like an earthquake. The sensation leaves me almost dizzy, but then my own anger takes over and chases away everything else. I grab onto it and let it take over. I need the anger to get through this discussion. Without it, I will turn into a weeping lump, and that won't do me any good.

I grab the papers from John's hand and try to keep them steady enough to read the words. Not an easy task. The papers are printed emails, just as Detective Swann said. My name, Phoebe Davidson, is clearly in the *from* line. The *to* line simply reads *Ron*

Carpenter. The date is June fourteenth. Only three days ago. The day of the murder. I swallow hard.

Impossible.

I quickly scan four more emails supposedly from me to the victim. The words become blurry as tears threaten.

Do not panic.

"There must be some mistake." I choke out the words. Breathing no longer feels natural. "I didn't send these. I didn't."

"I would like a few minutes to speak with my client. Alone." I feel John's arm move around my shoulders. Detective Swann raises his hands and gestures toward us. The move almost looks like a bow, like he's taking his kudos for finally finding some damning evidence against me. I look at Logan as well. His eyes meet mine directly. I've been avoiding eye contact with Logan, not wanting to feel the weight of his glare. Instead I'm greeted with different eyes, the same eyes from the night of the murder, eyes that are full of sympathy and understanding. I suck in a breath of surprise. Then my glimpse is gone as he turns his head away from me and walks out of the room, closing the door behind him.

My tears release as I fall into John. His arms go around me gingerly, like he's almost afraid to touch me. It's absolutely nothing like when Logan held me.

Is it part of a lawyer's job to console his clients? Whether it is or not, John comforts me as sadness fills me, and I sob into his dress shirt. He lets me cry for some time before he finally prompts me.

"They will only give us so much time. We have to spend at least a little of it actually talking about the case."

I sit up slowly. John hands me a handkerchief. A real one, made of cloth and everything. His initials *JEJ* are embroidered in the corner in navy thread. I carefully dab the tears from my cheeks, inhale a big sniffle, and hand it back to him. I don't dare blow my nose into something that looks so dainty.

"I didn't send those emails. Someone must have hacked into my email account. Or Detective Swann is trying to frame me. He thinks I'm guilty, so he's trying to find some way to prove it."

John sits up straight and tall. "Whoa there. Settle down. You can't go throwing around accusations like that."

"Go with my first theory then. There has to be some explanation because I didn't send those emails."

John reads the five emails out loud one by one. They are all short and to the point. In all of them, I'm trying to entice Ron Carpenter to come over to my house. I start out with a simple invitation to come over to my home to *talk*, the word is in quotation marks. I ask him not to respond to me, to keep up the mystery and that I will be in touch again soon.

Each email after that gets a little spicier, all with the same request that he not reply, that the fantasy must continue until we can be together. Two of the emails show pictures of me in a bikini. They were taken last summer when I went to Virginia Beach with my family. They aren't suggestive, but in this context, they're embarrassing.

The last email asks him to meet me at my house at nine o'clock on Monday night—the night of the murder. The one night in the last month that I've been on a date. Shoot, that was the one night in the last six months that I've had a date. Can't be a coincidence.

A quick rap on the door is the only warning we have before the detectives file back into the room. Logan's face is grim, his eyes are on the floor. Detective Swann is smiling.

This is not good.

They both take their original seats. Logan still won't look at me. He focuses on the paperwork in front of him.

"So, Ms. Davidson, now that you've had a chance to reacquaint yourself with your emails, would you like to admit that you knew Ron Carpenter?" Detective Swann's tone drips with condescension.

John jumps in. "Ms. Davidson is quite sure that she *did not* send these emails. It is entirely possible that her email account was hacked, and these emails were sent by someone else."

The corners of Detective Swann's lips curve even higher and take on a strained, even creepy feel. Nausea hits my stomach as if it's been thrust upon me. I take a deep breath and lean forward on the table, supporting myself with my elbows. I sneak a peek at Logan—he's still staring at his paperwork—before turning my attention back to Detective Swann, waiting for whatever bad news he's about to impart.

"We looked into the possibility of someone hacking Ms. Davidson's email account. All of these emails were sent directly from the IP address assigned to her computer. They were sent from her laptop, which she has said herself no one else uses."

"There has to be some other explanation. There has to be." My words are pleas at this point. Pleas that they will listen to reason. "I know that it looks bad, but I didn't send the emails. I didn't invite him over."

"Right, Ms. Davidson. You're just perfectly innocent, aren't you?"

"*I am perfectly innocent.* I wasn't even home when the murder happened."

"That's right. You were not home then. You made sure you were conveniently away from home, while your accomplice stabbed Mr. Carpenter."

My accomplice?

"No."

Detective Swann stands. "Ms. Davidson, you are under arrest for the murder of Ron Carpenter." His words barely register before the room begins to spin. John is speaking to me. I can see that his mouth is moving, but I can't hear anything he's saying over the whirring in my ears.

A uniformed policeman appears at my side. John stands and supports my elbow as I clumsily stand as well. I lean onto the edge of the table as I watch the lips of the policeman move. I catch a few words of what he's saying.

Arrest.

I'm under arrest.

This can't be happening. I don't even bother to look at Logan. He's behind me now and obviously no longer on my side in this nightmare.

***

They didn't handcuff me. I realize that now as I sort of *wake up* from the experience. I'm in a jail cell, an actual jail cell with bars and everything. Fortunately, I'm alone in my little room. There is an older gentleman in the cell next to me. He came in a while ago, belting out a tune from *The Phantom of the Opera*, but he apparently only knows a few words because he just kept singing *The Phantom of the Opera is there, inside your mind,* over and over again until the words began to fade and were finally replaced with rhythmic snoring.

There's no way I can sleep here. My mind is too busy whirring with the details of my nightmare. Those emails were sent from my laptop. *My actual laptop.* The only explanation is that someone came into my home and used my computer to send them.

How can that be? Someone had to have stolen my house key from my parents' home a while ago. They used the key to come into my home each day to send an email, and then they used it to come in my house to murder poor Ron Carpenter.

That's far-fetched. I don't even know if I would believe me, but I have thought of nothing else that would explain this. It's either this, or I have two personalities. I would know if I had two personalities, right?

Who would do such a thing?

I don't have any enemies. Do I?

My mind flashes with the look on my mother's face when she saw me being escorted by the policemen. Dad yelled something about bail, but the words didn't register. My only knowledge of this kind of thing comes from television. Sure I was arrested once before, but the charges were dropped right away, and I was never actually in a jail cell, just an interrogation room. I think that the judge has to agree to let me out on bail until my court date. The judge has to be awake for this to happen, so I'm likely in here for the night. I would rather stay here anyway than risk a judge being woken up in the middle of the night and being grumpy for his decision on whether or not to let me have bail. And hopefully he decides on an amount of money that my parents can afford. They aren't loaded, but they have their land. Will they have to use their farm as collateral? *Oh gosh.*

The sick feeling returns to my stomach. I eye the stainless steel toilet across from me and swallow hard. I can't actually *use* that toilet for anything. I'm definitely not *going* in it. I guess I will puke in it if I have to, but so far I've been able to fight back the sickness when it comes on.

I lie back down on the bench seat and hug my arms to me. It was only a few hours ago that Logan and I were in the throes of passion. That's not a phrase I would have used about myself in the past, but that's definitely what it was. Me? Against a wall? In such a hurry that there was no time to take our clothes off? My body breaks into a sweat from the memory of it all.

Now Logan won't even look at me. I thought that he believed in my innocence, but it's clear he doesn't any longer. He thinks I lied to him. How do I prove to him that I haven't lied? How do I prove to everyone that I'm innocent? If the police think I'm guilty, then it will be up to me to prove otherwise.

Chapter Twenty

Logan

No sleep for me tonight.

I can't stop thinking about the look on Phoebe's face when she was arrested. Her pleas of innocence seemed so sincere. But everything points to her guilt. Those emails—damning evidence for sure. Plus, the stabbing happened in her house. The evidence points to Phoebe being in on this.

So, why can't I shake the feeling that something is wrong? Why do I keep looking for things that don't add up? Is it because I care about Phoebe, and I *just know* that she can't be involved in anything like this?

She's innocent.

I know it.

Or is this exactly how she planned for me to feel

when she seduced me? Could she be that manipulative, that good of an actress?

She's not an actress.

She's innocent.

I give up on any hope of rest and move to the living room. My apartment is small, and even though I've been here a short time, it's easy to navigate through the darkness. I don't own much furniture, so there are not many hazards to trip over. I find the remote and power up the television. I settle for ESPN and the umpteenth replay of Sports Center.

It doesn't matter what's on. All I can think about is Phoebe and what an ass I've made of myself. A picture flashes into my mind of what happened between us just before Swann's phone call. *Wow*. Then I had to wall up every personal thought of her. I never would have made it through the interrogation if I was thinking of her in any way other than as a suspect. I could barely look at her during that interview.

But now that I'm alone in the dark, I can't *not* think of Phoebe and how she felt next to me, how it felt to be inside her. Perspiration covers my forehead as I remember us together. I have never *needed* like that. Needed Phoebe to be mine. Needed Phoebe at that instant. It's a frightening realization. Why her?

It's not just the *together* thoughts. It's afterwards, too. The perfect smile that was on her face as we lay together on her floor catching our breath. That smile was more than perfect teeth and full, pink lips. Her face was flushed, and her eyes were bright. It was like I could see through those beautiful blue eyes, right into her soul.

It was not the soul of a killer.

I completely overreacted when I received that phone call.

What the hell do I do now?

Chapter Twenty-One

Phoebe

Other than the complete humiliation surrounding the occasion, spending the night in jail wasn't as bad as I thought it would be. I didn't have to look tougher than I am, or get a burly girlfriend for protection, or even take up smoking cigarettes. *I really do watch too much television.* I guess I should count my blessings that there weren't more criminals arrested last night in Hickory Grove because when morning comes, it's still just me and the tenor in the cell next door.

A very nice woman, Ellen, brings me a cup of coffee and a sausage biscuit around seven-thirty. Her shoulder-length hair is dyed a platinum blonde and is styled to curl up and out on the ends. I say it's dyed, because she looks to be in her fifties and there's not a grey hair to be seen. She has round hazel eyes that compliment her kind, round face and plump, round body. She fusses over me some with a *tsk tsk* here and there, and she even lets me use the *real* bathroom down the hall. I have to have a police escort wait outside, but at least I am able to relieve myself. Holding my bladder was getting downright painful. I was actually starting to consider using the toilet in my cell. Desperate times call for desperate measures.

I can only handle a few bites of my breakfast, and that's fine. I just want to get out of here.

"You definitely aren't the type I usually see in here." The words spoken so close by cause me to start. I look up and see Opera Man staring down at me. He's very tall, well over six feet. His hair is silver, and he wears it pulled back in a ponytail. The hair of his unkempt beard is lighter than on his head, almost white. His eyes are a light grey, almost matching the color of his hair. There is a lot of pain in his look.

"What are you in for?"

I'd rather not tell anyone about this, but now that I've been arrested there will be no hiding it. "They think that I killed someone, but I didn't do it." My eyes immediately fill with tears. Saying the words out loud is difficult.

"No offense, but you're about as much a murderer as I am a heart surgeon."

"Thanks for that."

"Well, it's true. I can tell that much by looking at you." I try to form a smile. I don't think I'm very successful, but it's something. "I'm Bob, by the way, Bob Hanson."

"I'm Phoebe. What are you in for Bob?"

"Being the town drunk, I 'spose. They take pity on me when I drink too much and let me sleep it off in here." I take in his khaki pants and t-shirt, both very wrinkled and even dirty in a few places. Is Bob homeless? How nice of the police to let him stay here sometimes. I guess Detective Swann isn't all bad.

"Did my singing keep you up last night?"

I smile a real smile this time, remembering him singing as if without a care in the world. "No. I couldn't sleep anyway."

"Sorry about that. I tend to belt out show tunes when I drink too much. My wife loved *Phantom of the Opera*. She played the soundtrack all the time. It isn't my thing at all, but she loved it. And when I get drunk, I get sappy and start singing. I can't help myself." Poor Bob.

"Your voice isn't bad, but it would help us all if you could learn more of the words." I look up to see Ellen's kind, brown eyes watching us through the bars. I didn't hear her approach. I stand, walk toward her, and slide the rest of my sandwich to her through the bars, leaving my hand on one of the bars for support.

"You need to eat, sweetie."

118

"I just can't eat any more."

"I know that I'm supposed to be a *professional* and not take sides, but what kind of a person thinks *you* are capable of stabbing someone? Honestly." Ellen curls her brow up.

"That's what I just said," Bob pipes in.

"Thank you, both of you." Ellen believes me. Bob believes me. Why can't Logan believe me?

Ellen puts her warm hand on mine. "Oh, honey. I have a good sense about these things. They should let me decide who is innocent or guilty. You are a good girl, that much is obvious. There are some people out there in the world that I know are guilty of something. I can just tell, and yet they're walking around, free as birds."

Now I have the image in my head of a bunch of criminals flying around. My mouth can't help but form a weak smile.

"You know, I think you were my grandson's teacher last year. You are a teacher, aren't you?" I nod. "Isaac Chesterfield?"

"Isaac was one of my very best students. He's very driven, and he gets along well with all the other children. You must be really proud of him."

Ellen's lips burst into a smile. She beams with pride. "He's something, our Isaac," she says with a wistful smile. "You get some rest now. You should be out of here soon." She turns to my sort-of cellmate. "Bob, you're out of here now."

Bob walks to the door of his cell and pushes it

open. It wasn't even locked. He's like that guy Otis on the Andy Griffith Show.

"Good luck to you, Phoebe."

"Good luck to you, too, Bob." He turns and walks down the hall with Ellen.

I sit down slowly on the bench, thinking about my new friend Bob and the smiling face of little Isaac Chesterfield and pray that this night in jail will not be the end of my teaching career. This is a small town, and news travels fast. Not only do I have to prove my innocence, but I have a time limit. The summer won't last forever, and I need to be acquitted and back in my classroom by the end of August. That gives me about two months. I hope that's enough time. I never thought that I would be in this situation to start with.

It's almost nine-thirty before an officer comes to my rescue. He unlocks my cell and walks me to the front of the building where John and my parents are waiting. It's clear from the sagging look of their faces that my parents didn't get any sleep either. Their arms move around me in a tight hug, and they just hold me. Hot tears fill my eyes. I squeeze them hard to try to make the sting go away. It doesn't help.

I lean back some and look at Mom. "How much was my bail? Did you have to use the farm as collateral?"

She pats my shoulder. "Let's not worry about that. The judge was lenient. He set it at fifty thousand dollars. We had enough in savings to cover it."

"Oh, Mom. I'm so sorry."

"We know you didn't do anything wrong. We would have ransomed the moon if we had to. I can't believe that my baby spent the night in this place."

"It's okay, Mom. It wasn't as bad as I thought it would be." I say this for their benefit. Although it wasn't *as bad*, it did suck.

***

John buys us breakfast at the truck stop. Mom sits across from me, a pained expression marring her face as she stares first at me and then at my still-full plate. I nibble on a biscuit, but that's all that I can manage. My stomach feels full and ready to reject anything that comes its way. I don't want to take any chances. Mom, on the other hand, is a power eater. She polishes off two biscuits with gravy and a huge slab of country fried steak, while John explains the process to us in general terms.

"First, there's the arraignment, which is set for next Friday. That's where you will plead *not guilty,* and we'll hear the official charges against you. I don't expect this to go far, Phoebe. The legal system is slow. They will figure out that you're not involved long before we get to jury selection." He smiles, but it's a little weak to give me any real encouragement. "I will do some research as well, and we'll discover how the emails were sent from your computer."

"I didn't send them. You know that." I know that I've said it a few times now, but I say it this time while looking John straight in the eye. Things turned a little crazy in the interrogation room last night, at least *I* think they did. I got a little loopy, and some of the details are fuzzy. "It's important to me that you know that."

John smiles, a real smile this time. "Trust me, Phoebe, I know that you aren't capable of being involved in anything like this."

"It's ridiculous," Dad pipes in.

"Is Phoebe in any danger?" Mom asks quietly. "We don't know who is behind this. These people are obviously dangerous. How can we keep Phoebe safe while the police figure this out?"

"I don't think that she's in any immediate danger," John answers. "But, it wouldn't hurt for her to stay with you or with Lilly and Kevin until the police figure this out."

A groan involuntarily escapes my throat. "I am sitting right here. You don't need to talk about me as if I'm not. I'm a big girl, you know." Mom folds her arms in front of her and pulls her bottom lip up in a pout. I sigh and continue in a softer tone. She looks like Madison when Lilly tells her there will be no dessert. "Look. I'm sorry. I know that we've all had a crazy night, and we're all a bit punchy. But, I'm going to stay at my own house, and I'm going to be just fine." Mom opens her mouth to speak, but I quickly continue. "I promise to keep the house locked up.

Kevin changed the locks on both doors, so whoever was in there can't get inside anymore. They aren't after me anyway. For all we know, they could be on a beach in Tahiti by now. I promise you, this crime had nothing to do with me."

"You can't say that," Dad chimes in. "The murder happened in your house. That alone doesn't mean anything, but those emails were sent from your computer, your very own computer. Someone wanted to frame you for this."

I sit up as straight as I can, take a deep breath, and try to look as confident as possible. I know that Dad is right. I agree with him. Someone put me in this position on purpose. But I don't want Dad to think that, or I'll never get to be alone, much less try to figure this out on my own.

Chapter Twenty-Two

Logan

T.G.I.F. Right. More like Totally Getting Intensely Fucked. I guess that could happen in a good way— and it recently has—but that's not what I'm feeling today. I'm most definitely fucked in the worst way.

This has been the week from hell. I'm used to sleep deprivation, but my brain isn't working today. It's working I guess, but it's busy focusing on Phoebe and not on what Swann just said. I've had to ask him to repeat himself several times. If he wasn't in such a great mood, I think he would have whacked me upside the head by now. Instead, he just shakes his head and makes another snide remark.

"*As I was saying,*" he continues. "We need to get over to the library to see if they recognize Ron Carpenter's photo." I look at him again, waiting for him to tell me why we would go to the library. "*Because that's where the emails to Mr. Carpenter were read.* Honestly Matthews, do you have shit for brains? What is with you this morning?"

Big sigh. He's right. My brain is toast. "I'm sorry. I'm exhausted. I was up all night thinking about this case."

Swann shakes his head. "You let her get to you, didn't you?"

"What do you mean?" I didn't even look at Phoebe. Could he tell that I have feelings for her?

"That woman and her ridiculous story about how someone must have broken into her house to send emails and her whole *I'm so innocent* attitude. Give me a break already. You don't buy her story, do you?"

"I agree that the evidence against her is pretty substantial, but it doesn't feel right. She doesn't seem capable of being involved in a murder."

Swann shakes his head in obvious disgust. "I don't know how you did things down there in Miami, but here in Hickory Grove, we don't solve cases based on our *feelings*. Get your head in the game Matthews. Now let's go."

***

I haven't been to a library in years. The scent of the books is the first thing that hits me when the automatic glass doors slide open. The second thing is the noise. I remember libraries to be quiet places, but this one is anything but. Children are everywhere. A nearby sign announces that *Reading Roundup* starts in ten minutes. How they are going to get all these kids corralled, quiet, and listening to a story is beyond me.

Jacobson, the lab guy, has gone through Ron Carpenter's phone and email accounts. We've confirmed that Ron Carpenter ran a fairly large drug distribution service for Hickory Grove. In addition to whatever walk-up business he had, he also took orders via email. We found all the emails that Phoebe supposedly sent to Mr. Carpenter in his account as well as several others that appear to be requests for plants. We've determined that those must be in code. It isn't wise to request heroin, but there are emails requesting two tulips and three roses. So, if we can break the code, and we're working on it, the people who sent the emails are busted.

We're at the library today because as tech savvy as Ron Carpenter was, he sent his emails from one of the computers here. It's hard to believe that he was too cheap to buy a computer. We think it's more likely that in his warped mind, he thought that using one of these gave him some anonymity. Yet, he used his own email address. The man doesn't seem to have been the sharpest tool in the shed.

The library is manned by three women. Two are full-time librarians who work here Monday through

Friday. I don't mean to stereotype, but if I saw these ladies on the street, I would know that they are librarians. Mrs. Barkley, who spends most of her time at the main desk, at least on the weekdays, is in her sixties. She has a soft face and a round body. Reading glasses hang from her neck on a beaded chain. She looks like the kind of grandma who takes no nonsense but makes great chocolate chip cookies.

Mrs. Barkley carefully studies the photo of Ron Carpenter. Her bracelet jingles, and I see that the charms are adorned with little faces. Yep, grandchildren. Not a surprise.

After several seconds of studying the photo, she puts her glasses on and looks some more. "He comes in just about every day and uses one of the computers. He doesn't check out any books."

"You're sure? Looks like a lot of people come in here to use these." I gesture to the five computers that line the wall behind me. "It's the middle of the morning, and they are all being used."

She nods. "I'm sure. Many people come in to use the free internet on a regular basis, but it's usually the same ones over and over."

"Did Mr. Carpenter ever speak with you directly? Was he ever with anyone?"

"He said *hello*, but that's it. I've never had a conversation with him, and I don't remember seeing him with anyone else."

"Thank you for your time ma'am."

We exit the library and head back into the

sunshine. The sun bakes my arms through my shirt. It's a scorcher.

"Why didn't Ron Carpenter ever write her back?"

"The emails told him not to." Swann looks at me like I've lost my mind.

"I know that they did but still. You get emails like that, and you don't check them out? You just show up for a booty call and expect to get laid? Don't you think he should have suspected foul play?" Swann just shrugs his shoulders.

"The other thing that bugs me is Jeffrey Phillips."

"We don't need him to establish Ms. Davidson's alibi. There were others who saw her at Barney's that night."

"I know, but don't you think it's odd that he seems to have disappeared? Maybe it was his job to get Ms. Davidson *out of the way* so that Ron Carpenter could be stabbed in her home." *Crap. I almost called her Phoebe. That would have been bad.*

Swann's bad attitude seems to be back. "Maybe he's *missing* because she did him in, too."

My mouth drops open. "You don't mean that."

"Why not? Maybe she didn't want him to talk."

I just shake my head. I have no other response. There's nothing that I can say to make Swann see reason.

Chapter Twenty-Three

Phoebe

I finally got away from my parents. It took some arguing in the parking lot of the diner, but I was finally able to leave with John. He dropped me off at the police station to get my car where I left it last night. I thanked him and gave him a hug goodbye. Is it appropriate to hug your lawyer? I've slept with the detective, Logan, so at this point hugging my lawyer seems like nothing.

I promised them all that I would go right home, and I will, but I have a stop to make first. It's Friday afternoon. If I don't do this now, then I won't have a chance to check it out until Monday. I pull my car into the parking lot of the bank that just opened in the new strip mall out by the highway. This is where Jeffrey Phillips, my date from that night, told me that he works.

It hit me last night while in jail. The police are following up on Ron Carpenter. No one has mentioned a thing about Jeffrey Phillips. Someone planned for me to be away from home on Monday night. If that logic holds, then Jeffrey Phillips has to be involved. Or the criminals could really just be that computer savvy that they hacked my Love Match account as well and saw that I would be out with Jeffrey at that time. Either way, a visit with Jeffrey is in order.

I spend a moment in my car with a hairbrush and compact. I brush my hands along my skirt to help smooth out some of the wrinkles. Hopefully people will think that the wrinkles are from normal wear and not from a night in the slammer. As much as it feels like it, I am not wearing a sash that says *I was in jail last night.*

The hairs on the back of my neck stand up again. I scan the parking lot looking for Logan's detective car. I don't know what his personal car is, assuming he has one. Is he watching me again? This has got to stop. It is really starting to creep me out.

A young woman greets me with a pleasant *hello* as soon as I enter the bank. She looks to be barely out of high school, but she's dressed professionally in a navy business suit and heels. I return her smile and ask for Jeffrey.

"I'm sorry, but we don't have anyone here by that name."

My brow furrows. "Jeffrey Phillips? He's a financial planner who's been working here since you opened this branch a couple months ago?"

"I'm sorry, but we have no one here by that name. Our resident financial planner is Tom Franklin. She gestures to the photo of a smiling bald man who's at least sixty. Would you like to meet him?"

I politely decline and return to my car on jelly legs. *What the hell?*

Jeffrey, *probably not even his real name*, was in on it. In hindsight, it makes sense. He was all charm throughout dinner. He appeared interested in what I had to say. He was polite. He laughed at my jokes. Then, during dessert, he put his hand on my knee. It seemed inappropriate at the time, but I removed it, and we laughed about it. It wasn't until he walked me to my car that he made his big pass. He kissed me goodnight, really pretty chaste as kisses go and then grabbed my breast. It was a *grab* for sure, not a caress or even a brush. It was more like a honk, and it was disgusting. I told him that I didn't appreciate it, and then I left and drove straight home.

Looking at the whole picture, I can see that it was his job to keep me out of my house for a certain amount of time and then make sure that I went home alone. That's exactly what he did.

***

Lilly meets me at my car before I can even get the door open. She grabs me in a tight hug.

"My sister, the convict." She smiles. "And Mom and Dad always thought *I* was the wild one."

"Ha ha. Can I use your computer?"

"Sure. Come on in."

I follow her into her kitchen. She sets a cup of coffee and a piece of chocolate cake in front of me. "You already ate all the Twizzlers. This will have to do."

I look at the dark chocolate cake dripping with ganache. "This'll do." I shovel in a large bite. Delicious.

I type in the web address for Love Match to check my dating profile. I haven't been on here in days. Not since the murder. Not since I met Logan.

Deep breath. I need to stay focused on the here and now. I can pine for Logan later, when I'm home and alone.

Jeffrey's profile is just like I remember it. There he is. There's his name. It doesn't say that he works at that bank, but he told me that he did. Everything looks exactly the same. What did I expect to find? Maybe that his information would be deleted? I quickly send John an email with what I've found out about Jeffrey. I give him my login information as well so he can check it out for himself. Maybe he has an investigator that he works with on these kinds of cases. Lawyers do that in the movies.

"So, did you ever find out what was up with

Detective Matthews?"

"What do you mean?"

Lilly's eyes tighten as she studies me. "What did he want when he came here the other morning?"

I shrug. "I don't know."

Act nonchalant.

I do try, but I can tell that I'm failing when I feel the heat begin to creep up my neck.

"You slept with him!" Lilly bursts out, a maniacal smile spreads over her face. Her eyes are wide with surprise.

"I..." I can't think of anything to say. I've never been able to lie to Lilly.

"You slept with him, and then he arrested you? Were you that out of practice?"

"Nice Lill, really."

Her arm slides around my shoulders.

"How did this happen? You just met him, right?" I nod. "He's a detective working on your case." I nod again. "How?"

"There's just something about him. I feel like we have this connection. It's like when he touches me...I don't know. I do know that we can't seem to keep our hands off of each other, which is new for me."

"You like him, don't you?"

I shrug. "Yeah. Well, I did until he arrested me."

"That sucks."

"Yeah. Don't tell Mom."

Chapter Twenty-Four

Logan

What the hell is she doing?

It's Friday night, and it's been one helluva week. I should be sitting on my ass in front of the television, downing beer after beer. Instead I'm following Phoebe around like a puppy dog. I expected to just watch her house from my car, parked on the street. I just wanted to make sure that she was okay. I now know better than to peek in her windows, and I did do that for a while, but when Phoebe drove away, I followed her. Now, here we both are, parked on Ron Carpenter's street. So far, she's just watching the house.

Please stay in the car. This is not the kind of neighborhood where Phoebe needs to be. Swann and I came here in the day time, and it was rough enough then.

Shit. Phoebe exits her car slowly and closes the door behind her. She walks up the walk to the Carpenter's front door. Toys litter the small lawn. Some of them have been there for some time as evidenced by the tall grass growing in those areas. Mr. Carpenter or his *lawn service* mowed around the tricycle and rubber ball instead of moving them out of the way.

Phoebe looks right and left and then rings the doorbell. There's no car in the driveway, but the lights are on inside the house, so it appears that someone is home. Phoebe looks around again. Can she feel me watching her, or is she afraid to be here at night? Maybe both.

The porch light comes on and then the door opens. Mrs. Carpenter stands in the doorway, a toddler in her arms. I exit my car quietly and move toward the house. I don't see any way for this meeting to go well.

"Mrs. Carpenter?"

"Who are you?" Flora Carpenter sneers. Her words are slightly slurred. She's at least drunk, maybe high as well.

"My name is Phoebe Davidson." *Crap. She used her real name.* "I wanted to tell you that I'm very sorry for what happened to your husband."

"You have a lot of nerve coming here. You're the one who killed my Ronnie."

Shit.

Flora Carpenter steps out onto the front steps, forcing Phoebe to take a step backwards. Mrs. Carpenter looks much the same as she did when Swann and I were here earlier this week. Her short, brown hair is a tangled mess. Her face is thin and elongated like the rest of her body, with the exception of her surgically-enhanced breasts, which are busting out of her extra small tank top. Her cut-offs are so short that part of her butt cheeks must be hanging out the back. Flora Carpenter's appearance is in stark contrast to Phoebe, who wears denim Capri pants and a fitted, but definitely not too small tank top, over her perfect, *real and all natural*, breasts. My mind sees them again through the lace of that ivory bra she has. *I love that bra.* My body heats at the thought of them until I force myself back into the moment.

"Mrs. Carpenter, I assure you that I am innocent. I had nothing to do with your husband's death."

"How am I going to raise my babies now? Who is going to provide for us?"

"I'm sorry to bother you, but I was just hoping I could ask you a few questions."

"Questions? You want to ask me *questions* at a time like this?"

"I was just wondering if your husband ever mentioned a man named Alan Little."

So that's what this is about? Phoebe isn't here to give her condolences. She wants to see if there's a connection between Ron Carpenter and her ex-husband.

"Please leave."

"Mrs. Carpenter. *Please*. I need to know what happened."

"Get out, or I'm calling the police."

"No need. I'm right here." I chime in as I jog toward the women. Neither look happy to see me. "Mrs. Carpenter, is this woman bothering you?"

"Yes," she answers with a smirk. "I don't want her here."

I don't have to be looking at Phoebe to feel her eyes bore a hole in the side of my head. I turn toward her, and I'm blasted by the heat of the anger she radiates in my direction.

"Please come with me, Ms. Davidson."

Phoebe turns toward Mrs. Carpenter. "I'm very sorry for your loss and for bothering you. I only meant to try to find out what really happened." She turns on her heels and power walks to her car, leaving me to follow her.

She doesn't speak to me.

She doesn't look at me.

She gets into her car and drives away. I follow, of course.

***

I catch up with Phoebe just before she gets to her front door, even though I have to sprint across her front yard to do it.

"Leave. Me. Alone." I place my hand on her forearm. I want her to turn around and look at me. She brushes it off and stands facing her door.

"Why are you following me?"

"I just want to be sure you're all right."

"No. You don't. Now stop stalking me." Her body is so tight. Her words are spoken as a threat.

"Phoebe, I know I screwed up, but I care about you. I can't stand not knowing how you are."

"If you cared about me, you would believe me when I tell you that I'm innocent."

"I do believe you."

"Well, you sure have a nice way of showing it."

She's right, and I know it. I've been a complete asshole.

She puts her key into the lock.

"Wait." She does, standing still, her hand still on the doorknob.

"Why did you go to Ron Carpenter's house?"

She sighs. "I wanted to see if there was some connection between him and my ex-husband. Alan is the only criminal that I know, and since he and Ron Carpenter were both into selling drugs, maybe there's some connection there."

"We are looking into this. You don't need to be the investigator."

She turns and faces me now. A tear slips down her cheek, and it takes all my self-control not to brush it away.

"Apparently I *do* need to investigate this myself.

No offense, but the police aren't exactly doing a bang-up job. You have spent too much time finding me guilty, while the real murderer is out there somewhere. Did you even know that Jeffrey Phillips, whoever he is, doesn't exist? He was in on it, too."

I nod. "We haven't been able to find him. That was our conclusion as well."

"So go investigate already, and stop following me."

"Why aren't you at Lilly's or with your parents?"

"I live here."

I want to tell her that she doesn't have to be so brave. She doesn't have to be alone. She could stay with me. I want to know that she's safe. I don't say any of these things.

"Goodnight, Phoebe."

"Goodnight."

With that, she turns away from me, opens her door, and steps inside. The clunk of the deadbolt echoes in the darkness.

Chapter Twenty-Five

Phoebe

It's important to me to be a self-sufficient person. I don't want to make a big deal out of trying to be brave. I want to actually *be* brave. That's a lot easier to do in theory. It's not so easy to feel brave now that I'm here alone in my house, where a man died. Fortunately, I am a strong person and stubborn enough to feign bravery until I actually get the hang of it. That's my hope anyway.

Seeing Logan was hard. My talk with Mrs. Carpenter was tanking, and if he hadn't jumped in to break it up, she may have tried to hit me. I saw her making a fist with her free hand. But she had her baby in the other. She wouldn't really have hit me. *I hope.*

That doesn't mean Logan should have butted in.

What was he even doing there anyway? Is that what it's going to be like now that I'm out on bail? The police will be watching me? I could feel them watching me *before* I was arrested though. Why was Logan watching me then?

I check every window and door three times, just to be really sure that they're locked. I even step into the kitchen to check the window over the sink. It wasn't enough to look at it from my safe perch in the dining room, I wanted to touch it with my fingers. I lie in bed for a few minutes listening to the sounds of my house and neighborhood. Luckily, it is only a few minutes before sleep mercifully overtakes me.

***

Sleep is an amazing thing. I wake up feeling a little groggy from so much of it, but I am no longer impaired by the cobwebs from my lack of it. And it's easier to feel brave when the sun is shining through my windows.

Three texts from Mom. One from my sister. I quickly text them back to let them know that I'm okay. It's so much easier to communicate with them via text, they both can talk on the phone forever. I am not a phone talker.

I'm still not up for making coffee in my own kitchen, and coffee is just what I need right now. I quickly dress in some shorts and a tank, grab my purse, and head out the door. It's a beautiful morning. The birds are singing and everything. The sun is warm on my skin. I smile to myself and then shudder. Does my happy, free feeling this morning have anything to do with being *in jail* yesterday?

The line for coffee is long. I assume that's normal. I've only been here a handful of times. I don't only avoid this place because I think my own coffee is just as good, but it's also because of Joy. Joy Rogers. Joy dated Alan from middle school until I started dating him my junior year. They seemed like the perfect high school couple. She was a hot blonde cheerleader, and Alan was the gorgeous quarterback. They would have been prom king and queen and gone on to marry and have two perfectly blonde children. So, of course, she hates me.

Her light blue eyes meet mine the instant that I walk in the door, but her smile doesn't falter. She turns back to her customer and continues with her happy chit-chat. I listen to her cheerful banter as I move up the line. *Still a cheerleader,* I think to myself. She doesn't miss a beat when it's my turn. She still keeps her smile as she asks for my order, but I don't get the questions about my family or work, or whatever else it is that she asks her customers. It's all business, and that's fine with me. She does wish me a good day, which is the probably the nicest thing *Her Perkiness* has ever said to me.

I'm just being handed my very large cup when Logan walks in. The surprise on his face makes it seem like he didn't follow me here. Who knows? As

142

soon as our eyes meet, I feel him as much as see him. It's like his life force hits me, and I feel the heat of the blast everywhere. He holds the door for me and then follows me out. We stand together on the sidewalk, just outside the shop.

"Did you sleep okay last night?" Logan finally asks.

"Yes. You?"

"Yeah." The shadows under his eyes are still there although not as prominent as they were last night. He's wearing dress slacks and a button-down shirt, his work attire.

"Are you working today? It's Saturday."

"I am." His mouth curves up to a hesitant grin. "I have an important case that I'm working on." I give him a little smile, and his smile grows to a real one. His eyes brighten. A flutter starts in the pit of my stomach and curls outward. *Stay strong. You are mad at him.* My brain issues the order, but I don't think my body is listening.

"What are you going to do today?" Logan asks the question as he fidgets with his collar.

"I'm not sure, actually. I'm still making a plan."

"Will you leave the investigating to me? Please?" I shrug. "I just don't want you to get hurt."

I have to admit, he seems sincere, even if I don't want to hear these words. But his show of concern has the opposite effect on me than he seems to have intended. The fluttering stops abruptly and falls to the pit of my stomach, reforming into a sea of anger.

How can he stand here and tell me he doesn't want me to get hurt? He arrested me.

"I'm fine, *Detective.*"

Logan grimaces but quickly recovers. He leans in close and speaks quietly in my ear. "You are not fine, Phoebe. I have been here for coffee every morning that I've lived in this town, and I have never seen you here. Do you suddenly have a hankering for gourmet coffee, or are you too afraid to make it in your own kitchen?"

I grit my teeth. "Does it make you feel better to insult me?"

"No." His quick breath travels across my ear. I'm torn between wanting to punch him and rip his clothes off. "Dammit, Phoebe. I care about you."

The anger beats away my lust, and I move away from him. "How can you say that? You arrested me, Logan. *Arrested.* I spent the night *in jail.*"

"I am truly sorry that you had to go through that. But, that's why I'm working today. I want to find the answers. I want to prove your innocence."

"Just leave me alone." I turn and walk to my car. *Very mature Phoebe.* When in doubt, walk away. I watch Logan watch me. With shaky hands, I put my car into reverse and back carefully out of my parking space.

Chapter Twenty-Six

Logan

I fucked up. I know I did, but what was I supposed to do? I'm a cop. On a case. That has to come first. My only hope is to figure this out and prove that Phoebe is innocent. If I can do that, then maybe I'll have a chance. Maybe I can make her understand.

The office is empty today. We only run a couple of patrol cars over the weekend—very low key—and they spend most of their time looking for speeders and answering domestic dispute calls. It will be good to get some work done without Swann breathing down my neck.

I boot up my computer and begin my research on Phoebe's ex-husband. There's plenty of information just from the local newspaper, even though it's distributed only once a week. Over a two-year period, there are seventeen articles. That's a lot of mentions for one person. I learn quickly that Little was the football star of the town. He was recruited by the University of North Carolina with a full scholarship. Interesting, but not what I'm looking for.

The marriage announcement came five years later. *Mr. And Mrs. Frederick Davidson announce the engagement of their daughter, Phoebe Davidson, to Mr. Alan Little, the son of Mr. and Mrs. David Little.* A sterile photograph of the couple accompanies the picture.

The next article is from six months later. It was a June wedding. *Of course it was.* It's a big spread with three photos. One of the photographs shows a typical wedding moment. Alan Little wears a tux. Phoebe wears a white dress. They stare into each other's eyes, smiles on their faces. Phoebe looks beautiful. Pangs of jealousy rip through me as I stare at the screen.

Deep breath.

Thank God Swann isn't here to see my reaction to this. He would know something is up for sure. I am literally sweating. My reaction provides even more motivation to get this case solved.

The remainder of the articles are all about Alan Little's arrest and trial. He was arrested for drug possession first—marijuana. It was a small amount, and as crimes go, not that big of a deal. That was just the tip of a very large iceberg. He was arrested again two months later for heroin possession. He paid a fine and went away to rehab. The article is a pretty soft piece depicting *poor Alan Little* and clearly showing pity for the Little family. A family photo had been included. Little, along with his parents and younger brother, are all smiles. It was taken earlier than the wedding photo though. I make a note of the reporter's name, Sam Hudson. It wouldn't hurt to talk to him.

The next article is not soft. Written only six months later, it paints a different picture of Alan Little. This time he was arrested for heroin possession with an intent to sell. The photo with this article is decidedly different as well. Little looks completely strung out. His eyes are wide and harried, his skin taut. His hair is a messy mop, as if it hadn't been combed in days. He looks like a completely different person than in the previous photos. I can only imagine what this asshole put Phoebe through.

The rest of my research shows that Little spent two years in prison outside of Richmond. He was well-behaved while incarcerated and was even released six months early. His parole officer hooked him up with a construction job, which he kept for three months. There's no record of him anywhere after that.

I make a call to the parole officer, Albert Fox, but learn nothing new. He thought that Little was on the straight and narrow. He made all of his meetings and was a good employee until his parole period ended. Then he just vanished. Fox told me that he wouldn't have known anything was amiss if he hadn't received a call from Little's boss. Little just never showed up for work one morning. The manager was used to the parolees skipping town—it happens—but he was pissed about Little leaving because he was such a good employee.

***

My first stop is the newspaper office. I would like to speak with reporter Sam Hudson. It's closed. Small town. He's probably out covering a quilting bee, whatever that is.

The Little family lives in one of the large, old homes on Main Street. A huge green carpet of grass provides a buffer from the road. I turn onto the driveway and listen to the gravel give under the wheels of my car.

The house has two levels with a large front porch that stretches across the entire front facade. Huge potted ferns hang across the front of the house. Black shutters—real, actual shutters—hang on every window. Wooden chairs line the porch, giving the place a formal feel. This is a porch built for a swing and some rocking chairs.

I fully expect the door to be opened by a servant. It isn't. I recognize Mrs. Little from the photograph included with the newspaper article. She is dressed in a nice blouse and slacks, pearls around her neck. I guess this is not a casual Saturday afternoon. I wonder if they have those here.

I introduce myself, and given the skeptical look she shoots me, I flash my badge. She invites me into her home, but once inside, she stands in the foyer and doesn't offer me a chair.

The foyer is as grand as I would expect it to be based on the outside of the home. The floors are oak planks as is the large staircase that rises in front of me. A huge crystal and brass chandelier hangs from the ceiling above me. The place is...uptight.

"To what do we owe the pleasure?" Of course. She wants to know why I'm here.

"I was wondering if you might be able to help me contact your son, Alan. I would like to ask him a few questions."

Mr. Little chooses this moment to walk toward us from the back of the house. He's dressed as I am. I hope that the Littles have somewhere to go this afternoon, but I get the feeling that this is just how they are.

"What's going on here?" he asks, his voice a deep baritone.

I turn and shake his hand. "Mr. Little, I'm Detective Matthews. I was hoping that you could help me contact your son, Alan. I just have a few questions for him."

"Do you know him?"

"No, sir."

"Is this about what happened at his *ex*-wife's house the other night?" Mrs. Little asks.

"Yes, ma'am. How did you know about that?"

"I heard about it when I had my hair done yesterday. It's all anyone could talk about. I always knew that Phoebe Davidson was trouble, but I never thought she would be capable of something this horrible." Mrs. Little makes a face when she speaks Phoebe's name, as if she's just tasted a Sour Patch Kid.

"What did you mean when you said that Phoebe Davidson was trouble? Everyone that I have spoken with has said nothing but good things about her."

"Phoebe Davidson is white trash," she says smugly. "Her parents are *farmers*. Did you know that?" I nod. "She may have cleaned herself up some, and maybe her sister married well, but you can't change who you really are. Other people don't know her like we do." Mr. Little puts his arm around her shoulders as if to comfort her from the terrible recollection of Phoebe. *This I gotta hear.*

"Our Alan was a football star. Did you know that?"

I nod. "I read several articles about his football career in the archives of the Gazette. Very impressive numbers."

"He got a full scholarship to UNC." Mr. Little's hand squeezes her shoulder.

"I read about that, too." *Go on.*

"Phoebe talked him out of going. She was a year behind him in school. She begged him to stay home. She said that she couldn't be without him. He didn't go. He didn't go away to school," she repeats, as if I didn't understand her words the first time. "Then, when she graduated high school she left him here. Can you believe it?" Tears fill her eyes. "He gave up everything for her, and then she left him without any thought." There has to be more to this story, but this is not the time to dig. "I'm not sure what Alan ever saw in Phoebe in the first place, but he stuck with her. She went away to James Madison University. He tried to get in as well, but no one wanted him a year later. He was left with taking classes at the community college. He worked hard and got his Associates Degree in Management and began working with one of our friends who has a construction business. We felt so badly for Alan. He gave up so much for her, and what did she care?" Mrs. Little wipes her eyes now, smearing a line of mascara under her eye. "We tried to talk some sense into him, make him see how toxic she was to his life. That didn't work. He visited her at college almost every weekend and then proposed to her before she even graduated."

"Were you against the marriage?" Seems obvious, but I can't help but ask.

"It was clear to us that Phoebe was what Alan really wanted, so we gave them our blessing and tried to put the whole nasty business behind us.

They were married about two years before the trouble happened. Alan fell in with the wrong crowd, the men he worked with were not the most savory bunch, and he got hooked on...*drugs*." She whispers the word as if it is too horrible to say out loud. "It was so shocking. We tried to get him help. We sent him to a place in Florida that specializes in that kind of thing. *She* didn't support Alan. As soon as Alan needed her, she left him. *She's the one who turned him in to the police, and then she left him*. What kind of support is that? It killed Alan. It's her fault that Alan went to prison. If Phoebe had been a good wife, the kind that stands by her husband, maybe Alan could have licked this. Instead she just left him when he needed her the most."

Mrs. Little is full-on crying now. Mr. Little pulls her into an embrace.

"I think you should leave now," he says sternly.

"Would it be possible for you to give me Alan's phone number? I would really like to speak with him directly."

"You don't think Alan has anything to do with this." Mr. Little is yelling now. His eyes are wild. "He's in California."

"No, I do not believe that he does, sir. Like I said, I just have a few questions that I'd like to ask him."

"We do not have a way of reaching Alan at this time," Mrs. Little says quietly. "Alan's job requires him to travel, so he contacts us when he can."

"When was the last time you spoke with Alan?"

"He called Wednesday evening. He is working with a construction crew in San Francisco."

I hand Mr. Little my business card. "When you speak with him again, would you please ask him to call me? It's really only a formality, but we'd like to make sure we have our bases covered."

"Thank you, Detective," Mr. Little announces.

"Thank you. Very nice to meet you both."

I show myself out the door and feel their glares stabbing me in my back as I walk back to my car.

Chapter Twenty-Seven

Phoebe

So far, this has been a huge waste of a day, and I really can't afford that right now. I'm just not sure what to do next. I spent the first part of the day trying to recall what I was doing on each day and time that I supposedly sent an email to Ron Carpenter. I didn't send them, so if they truly were sent from my computer, then the only explanation I have is that someone snuck into my home and sent them while I was away.

There were five emails, and they were sent at different times of the day. The first was sent last Thursday at 1:43 pm. I ran some errands that afternoon to the bank and the grocery store. Maybe I'm on their surveillance cameras, or better yet, there has to be a record of my debit card purchase. I make a note on a sticky, and attach it to the email.

The next email was sent on Friday at 12:47 pm. I remember this. I had lunch with my friend Melody. We went to Barney's. They should take Melody's word for that, but even if they don't, someone at Barney's should remember me. I note everything and stick it on the email.

Saturday at 2:25 pm. That one is easy. I was at the pool with Lilly and the girls. We were there all afternoon and then had grilled burgers at their house. Will Detective Swann believe my family as an alibi? If not, that will be a problem for Sunday as well. Sunday's email was sent at 4:59, just as we were sitting down to a family dinner at my parent's house. That's our Sunday tradition. I'm there every Sunday night for dinner at five sharp. I read Sunday's email again, and the nausea hits me hard. The emails before this one were suggestive. This email is the first one that comes right out and promises explicit sexual acts.

Then there's the one from Monday that not only makes more promises but begs him to be at my house, *my house*, at nine o'clock. In the note, I supposedly tell him to park down the street and come in through the back door, where I will be waiting for him in the kitchen. Instead, someone else was waiting for him, waiting to end his life. I shiver at the thought.

Who would want him dead so badly? Who would want to implicate me in the murder? I don't think I have any enemies. Sure there are people who don't like me very much, but I can think of no one who actually *hates* me.

I did try the last phone number that I have for Alan. The message on the voicemail that came on was female and young and definitely not Alan. I would assume that his parents know how to reach him, but they will have to be a last resort. They hate me.

I try to remember a couple of the names mentioned at the time of Alan's arrest. Bart and Carla Higgins are the only ones that come to mind. So much was coming at me at that time. I thought I knew who Alan's friends were, but there was a whole part of his life that I didn't know about. I kept many of the newspaper articles and read through them over and over in the beginning. I finally made myself burn them. *Yes, I actually burned them.* It seemed more final that way. Now, I wish that I still had them, so that I could have a clue as to what to look for next.

Bart and Carla Higgins were arrested with Alan. They were a team, the three of them. They all went to prison around the same time. Maybe I can get some ideas from Bart and Carla.

My computer hasn't been returned to me, and it's difficult to do research without it. So, that's why I find myself at Lilly and Kevin's. I can't go to Mom and Dad's. They would ask too many questions. Lilly will ask questions, too, but her questions will be about Logan. Both options suck. I debate going to buy a new computer, but I finally decide to suck it up and go to Lilly's. Maybe I'll get lucky, and she will be with the girls at a birthday party or something.

No such luck. Of course not.

Hillary and Maddie run out the door to greet me. I squat down and brace myself for impact. They hug me so tightly, and for three whole seconds, life is wonderful. They each take one of my hands and pull me toward the house.

The hairs on my neck prickle. Someone, probably Logan, is watching me...again. This is getting so old. I don't have time to dwell on it because the girls start talking. Their little voices speak over each other excitedly, giving me all the news of their lives in a rush of words.

"Miss Kathy said that we are going on a field trip to a potato chip factory. *My friend Jane got a horse.* I love potato chips. *A horse!* Don't you love potato chips, Aunt Phoebe? What's your favorite kind? *She said that I can ride her sometimes.* Mine is barbeque, and I also like the sour ones, I can't remember what they're called. *She named her Annie. If I had a horse, I would name her Sky. Don't you think that's a good horse name*? Daddy likes the plain ones. How boring is that?" It's a constant stream of words, with no pauses whatsoever for me to answer any of their questions.

Lilly is waiting for us on the porch. "Ladies, give your Aunt Phoebe a break. Finish up your lunch, and

Daddy will take you to the pool." The shouts of glee carry through the house as they run toward the kitchen.

Lilly pulls me into a hug. "I wish I had half their energy."

"Tell me about it. Lately, it's like they're so wound up, they're going to pop. I took the morning shift and let Kevin sleep in, so he owes me. Come have a seat, and fill me in on what's been happening."

"Can I use your computer first?"

"I was hoping we could have some sister time."

"We can, maybe while you help me with something?"

***

Bart and Carla Higgins live on Blossom Street in a not great but not horrible part of town less than a mile from Lilly and Kevin's wealthier neighborhood.

"I can't believe we live so close to drug dealers." Lilly has repeated this sentence several times since she found out what I wanted to do for our sister bonding time.

"They might not be drug dealers anymore," I say again in a voice that isn't even convincing to myself. "Besides, I lived *with* a drug dealer and didn't know it. You never know."

This street is much nicer than where the Carpenters live. The Higgins home has a yard that is mowed, like all the way, without splotches of taller grass dotting the landscape. The house looks freshly painted, and there's a newer model Ford pick-up parked in the driveway. I park my Civic on the street and study the house a little more. Lilly studies me. While she says she understands my need to prove my innocence, she acts like I'm cuckoo for Cocoa Puffs.

"Let's get this over with." My words are not exactly confidence-inspiring, but I don't have a lot of practice at this sort of thing either.

We exit the car and move up the walkway. I hold my head high, like I belong here. I'm not trying to sneak in or break and enter. I just want to talk to them. The door opens before we reach the front steps.

"Well. Well. Well. If it isn't Rich Bitch Little." The woman speaking is Carla Higgins. I remember her picture from the mug shot printed in the newspaper. She looks much better now. Of course, most people probably look better in real life than in their mug shots—*I hope I do*—but Carla looks much better. Her face is fuller, her eyes not so sunken in. She's dressed in a comfy-looking pair of shorts and a t-shirt. Her long legs are tan, which is a feat considering it's only June. She looks healthy and definitely *not* like a drug dealer. What do I know, though? I didn't think Alan looked like a drug dealer either.

"I'm very sorry to bother you, but would it be okay if I ask you a couple questions?"

"No." Her facial expression doesn't change. She just answers *no* very matter-of-factly.

"I promise that it will only take a minute or two of your time."

"Still used to getting everything you want, Rich Bitch? Don't know what the word *no* means?" I sneak a look at Lilly. Her body is taught, her hands are fisted at her sides. Does she think we're going to get in a fight or something? I guess I should have brought Lilly with me the other night when I visited Mrs. Carpenter. I need to defuse this situation now.

"Why do you keep calling me that?" I try to sound calm and non-threatening. It's a reasonable question. "I'm not rich, I'm not a bitch, and I definitely don't get everything I want."

"Alan told us all about you. I don't know why he stayed with you. We tried to talk some sense into him but never could. Alan was good to you, working hard to give you all the things you wanted, and what did you do in return? You spent every dime that he gave you, and then you turned him over to the Feds. Bart and me, we did our time. We got a good life now, and we want nothing to do with you or Alan either for that matter. Now get the hell off my property."

I carefully grab Lilly's forearm, I figure slow movements are best right now.

"He was a drug dealer." *Which probably doesn't make sense to another drug dealer.* I take one step backwards and pull Lilly back with me. But, I can't leave with nothing. I have no other leads.

"Does the name Ron Carpenter mean anything to you? Did Alan know him?" I throw it out there and get a reaction. Carla's eyes widen. Her mouth opens slightly before she realizes it, but she quickly purses her lips together. *Too late.* "Was Ron a friend of Alan's?"

"Hardly." Carla takes a step toward us. "I asked you to get off my property."

"Thank you for your time." Lilly and I both turn and power-walk back to my car. I feel again like I'm being watched, but I see no one around. When I turn back and look at the Higgins's house, I see no one watching us from there either.

Chapter Twenty-Eight

Logan

"Are you here in an official capacity?"

Phoebe does not look happy to see me. She stands in her doorway, only allowing the door to open enough for her to peek out at me. She eyes me skeptically, her lips pursed tightly. I miss the amused look she had when Arnie busted me the other night. It's my own fault, but I'd still really like to see it again someday. *Who am I kidding?* What I'd really like to see is the look of contentment she gave me after what we did against her dining room wall. That's something that I would like to see again someday.

Such an idiot.

"What do you mean?" I ask as innocently as possible, knowing perfectly well what she means.

"Well, it's still daylight, and you're knocking on my door in plain sight for all the neighbors to see. Do I need to call John so that he can be present for this *interview,* or did you take a second job delivering pizzas?"

"This is a peace offering," I say, holding up the pizza and executing a slight bow. "You can call John if you'd like, but I want to talk with you about Alan."

"You're going to have to do better than a pizza." One hand goes to her hip. The other is planted firmly on the door, holding it mostly closed.

"I know." I look down at my feet. I can't help it. "Think of it as the first of many gifts. Can I please come in?"

"On one condition."

"What is that?"

"You have to stop following me." My eyes pop up to meet hers.

"What do you mean, following you?"

"Just like at the Carpenter house last night. And then today at my sister's, and then when I was talking to Carla Higgins. I don't want you following me around. I want you working on my case, proving my innocence."

"Why do you think that I'm following you?"

"Well, you were there last night. But besides that, I can just feel it. I know when I'm being watched."

Shit. Who is following Phoebe? Could it be Swann? I really don't think so. He told me he was going fishing this weekend. He and Mason were talking about it in the office yesterday. I turn and look up and down the block. Mine is the only car parked on the street. The rest are parked neatly in driveways. Nothing seems out of place.

"Do you feel like you're being watched right now?"

"No, but you're standing right in front of me. That's different than when you watch me from down the street or wherever you are."

"Let me come inside, and we will talk about it."

"I think I can come up with alibis for every one of those emails." She says the words as a challenge.

"That's good, but I'm not here to talk to you about the emails. We can talk about those with Swann on Monday. Please let me in."

Phoebe steps to the side and opens the door enough for me to enter. I carry the pizza to her kitchen and set it down on the counter. Maybe it's a mean trick, but I want to see if she'll follow me into the kitchen or not. She does. She walks an awkward circle around the room to avoid the spot in the middle of the floor where Ron Carpenter died, but she does walk into her kitchen. She grabs two plates from a cabinet and hands one to me. We both get a slice of pizza and a beer, and then I follow her back into the living room. Her short shorts afford a nice view of her long, shapely legs. My body instantly responds. I concentrate on my breathing and try to look elsewhere as I take the seat next to her on the couch. *The couch.* The one where things started the other night.

It's clear from Phoebe's body language that she won't be jumping my bones tonight. She sits about two feet away, careful not to touch me this time. Her thighs are pressed together tightly, seemingly to provide level support for her plate, but it could also be a signal whether conscious or unconscious, to stay away from her.

I take a big pull from my beer.

"Should you be drinking while on the clock?"

I set the bottle carefully on a coaster and turn toward Phoebe. "I'm making this visit *off the clock*."

"How do I know that?" She doesn't look at me when she speaks. She seems to be focused on her slice of pizza, but from the look of things, I doubt that she even sees it. Her hands press tightly into the couch cushions on each side of her body. I reach out and carefully remove the plate from her lap. She still doesn't look up. "You are a detective. It's a part of you, and you can't help that."

I can't believe what I'm hearing. I thought I would never get Phoebe to understand that about me, and here she is, saying the exact words I was going to say to her. My body tingles with the beginnings of immense relief. I lean forward and tip her jaw lightly so that she can look at me. She keeps her eyes downward.

"Phoebe." Her eyes lift at the sound of her name, and they find mine. "What you say is exactly true. I am a detective, and being a detective makes me question everything. I can't change that. I'm so very sorry though for having hurt you. The detective in me was overwhelmed by the evidence, but I do believe that you're innocent. Let me prove it. Let me prove to you that I'm worthy of your trust."

"I understand that you are a detective, and you have to check out the evidence, but what hurt the most is that you doubted me so quickly. We had just had what was beyond a doubt the hottest sex of my life. Doesn't that count for something? We could share something so intense, so intimate, and then the way you looked at me." Tears slide down Phoebe's cheeks. She doesn't make a move to wipe them away, so I do. My fingertips brush gently against her cheeks.

"You're right. I was almost in shock when Swann told me about the emails. I felt so betrayed."

"*You felt betrayed*?" Disbelief echoes in her tone. I quickly try to explain.

"I was wrong. I was afraid that you had used me, that you made me have feelings for you." She looks at me like I'm insane. I shrug. "That's what I felt like at the time. I knew as soon as I left your house that I was wrong. I wish I could take it back."

"Logan, *you arrested me*. I spent the night *in jail*."

"I know." I take her hands in mine and squeeze them tightly. She doesn't pull away from me. *Thank you, God.* This is more relief than I should feel about this situation. I know that I should keep away from her, but I can't. I just can't *not* touch her. "I didn't have a choice about arresting you. The evidence. Those emails. They look really bad."

"You told me that you were going to remove yourself from this case, but you didn't."

"*I couldn't.* I can't. Swann thinks you're guilty, and he's trying to prove it."

Phoebe pulls away from me, stands, and paces in front of her coffee table. "What about being innocent until proven guilty? What happened to that?"

"The system will work. Let me do my job, and the truth will come out. I know you, and you didn't stab that man."

Chapter Twenty-Nine

Phoebe

"How do you know that? *You don't know me.* We just met." Logan's eyes widen in surprise. I'm surprised at myself, as well. I've been trying to convince Logan of my innocence, and now I argue with him when he agrees with me. "It doesn't matter anyway. I was with Alan for almost ten years, and I didn't know him." I hug my arms across my chest.

Logan stands and walks to me. His warm arms wrap around me. He smells of sunshine and cologne. He plants a soft kiss on my temple.

"Phoebe, I know that you aren't capable of committing murder."

I sigh heavily as I move my arms across the starched smooth cotton of his dress shirt and hold them together behind his back. I hold on tightly.

With his words come a feeling of weightlessness. *He believes me.*

Logan pulls away enough for our eyes to meet. "Is Alan capable of stabbing someone?"

"I want to say *no*, but I wouldn't have thought Alan capable of drug trafficking." I chew on my bottom lip, unsure what I should say about Alan, but I have to say something. "I think Alan knew Ron Carpenter."

"Did Alan speak of him?"

"No. I didn't know about any of Alan's *associates*. He kept that part of his world hidden. But Carla Higgins had a reaction to Ron Carpenter's name. I don't know what Alan told her about me, but Carla wouldn't tell me anything."

"She wouldn't tell me much either, but this town isn't very big. Ron and Alan were both in the drug business. They had to know each other. The question is whether they worked together or were rivals. That's what we need to figure out, and since Carla Higgins didn't give either of us any information about that, we will have to find someone else to ask." Logan pauses and watches me for a moment. "Carla did mention that you were there earlier in the day, and it was pretty clear that you are far from her favorite person."

A chuckle escapes from somewhere inside me. This isn't something to laugh at. I think it's more like hysteria. Logan moves his arms to my shoulders and squeezes lightly.

"You have to stop trying to investigate this case by yourself. These are not nice people. You're going to get hurt." His tone is soft, but his words are like the screech of fingernails down a blackboard. If I'm nothing else, I'm stubborn.

"No."

"No?" His arms drop to his sides.

"I can't just sit around and watch Detective Swann put me in jail for good. I have to stand up and fight." Logan's mouth opens slightly—I assume to argue with me—but he smartly closes it. "Besides the obvious fact that I need to prove my own innocence, I need to know if Alan is involved. I *have* to know."

"Have you eaten anything today?"

I shake my head. "Just the coffee this morning."

"That's what I thought. You look exhausted. Come sit down and eat your pizza. I know it isn't exactly healthy, but it's something." I feel Logan's hand move to the small of my back as he guides me toward the couch. This time he sits a little closer, and I let him. There will be no more sex until this is over, but even so it's nice to have him close to me.

I take a bite of pizza and chew it slowly. It's cold now, but it's still delicious. We only have one non-chain pizza place in town, and their pizza is extraordinary.

"I tried to call Alan this morning." I throw the words out there. I was unsure how to bring up the fact that I'm trying to find him. We were just talking about Alan, and it makes sense that it's part of the investigation, but it feels odd to talk about him with Logan.

"Were you able to reach him?"

"No. It was an old phone number. I wanted to see where he is, to see if he was anywhere in the area."

"His parents say that he's in California."

I can't stop the quick intake of breath. Logan notices. He doesn't miss much. "You spoke with the Littles?" He nods. Of course he did. "They hate me."

Logan shrugs. "I've heard their side of the story. Why don't you tell me yours?"

***

"Alan was the all-out king of our high school—geez, maybe even the whole town. Everyone knew Alan Little, and those who didn't know him personally wished that they did. He was a football hero, and his family is still one of the most prominent in town. He was dating Joy Rogers, and everyone thought they made the perfect couple. Even I thought that they did." I pause and look at Logan. His eyes are focused. His brow is creased, showing his concentration. He's listening intently. I can't help but wonder if he wants to know about Alan as a man or as a detective. Maybe both. I focus again on my partially eaten piece of pizza and continue."

"I was working on the school newspaper and

was assigned the job of interviewing Alan on the Monday after a big game. College scouts had seen him play, and he'd performed perfectly. We sat on Alan's front porch. Alan wore his team jacket and looked like the epitome of the small town football hero. Confidence oozed from every pore of his being. All that confidence somehow made me feel stronger, too. It felt good to be there with him."

"I studiously asked him questions and wrote down every word he said. I knew that he was taken, everyone knew, but I couldn't help thinking how great it was to have this time alone with him. I knew that under normal circumstances, Alan Little would never give me a second look." I pause, remembering that day. There was a chill in the air, but it wasn't cold yet, just a hint of the winter to come. Alan smiled at me with this amazing smile. It was crooked on one side, his perfectly white teeth shining through. He was beautiful. I tried not to look at him too much, so instead I concentrated on a nearby maple tree. The bright yellow leaves were raining down on the green grass below.

"I was totally surprised when Alan kissed me, just out of the blue. I did not see it coming." I sneak another look at Logan. His eyes show that his mind is busy at work, but what is he thinking about? Is he picturing the moment? Is there any jealousy there? *Do I want Logan to be jealous*? Is he trying to gauge my truthfulness? I don't want to be under his microscope, but I need to tell him this story. I look away from Logan and let my eyes settle on my beer bottle.

"I was shocked. I couldn't believe that the captain of the football team had just kissed me. He said all these incredibly sweet things *to me* and then asked me out on a date the next Friday night, after the football game. I asked him about Joy, and he said that they were pretty much over. He said that he would officially end it, and he wanted to go out with me. *Me.* I just kind of nodded and never really believed that anything would come of it. But it did. It was very fairy tale, and I couldn't believe that it was happening to me."

I take a long pull from my beer without looking at Logan. I feel so foolish when I think back on that time. *Fairy tale.* It did feel magical at the time and look what a nightmare it turned out to be. Alan was never *mine.* I had to share him with the entire flipping town. Everyone seemed to think their opinion mattered. Tears threaten, but I push them back. I'm not allowing myself to shed one more tear for Alan.

"If I was surprised by this turn of events, it was nothing compared to what other people thought. Alan's family loved Joy and never missed an opportunity to talk about her in front of me. Mrs. Little still took Joy shopping and stayed in touch with her. I think she thought that I was temporary and that Joy would be the woman Alan married.

Joy, of course, hated me right away. I can't say

that I really blame her for it. I would feel the same way if I were in her shoes. There were all kinds of rumors about me after that. I can only assume that Joy and her friends were behind most of them. *That* I wouldn't have done. I would have hated her in silence and complained to my friends. That would have been the extent of it." I look up at Logan now. His eyes are still sporting the same curious stare. "And just so you know, *Joy* is the woman you get your coffee from every day. She's the reason I avoid the coffee shop."

Logan nods understanding and then asks, "The Littles said that Alan didn't go away to school because he wanted to stay here with you. Is that what happened?"

"Yeah. They blame me for that. I didn't tell Alan to stay here. I actually encouraged him to take his scholarship. I knew that we would be apart, but it was the best thing for him and for us in the long run. I didn't want him to give up his dream for me. I thought we would have years to be together. But Alan insisted on staying here to wait on me. Then, when it was my turn to go to college, he was pissed that I left. I worked my butt off for my scholarship, and it was just a partial. I had to work two jobs to put myself through school. My parents helped a little, but they didn't have that kind of money. I couldn't give up on my dream just because Alan did. He said that he planned to go to school with me when I went, but I don't think that he ever actually wanted to go. I mean, he said that he got rejections from the schools he applied to. That could be true, but I never actually saw any letters. It just seems kind of fishy. I have come to the conclusion that maybe it was more Mr. Little's dream that Alan be a football star."

"They blame me for turning Alan in to the police, too." Logan nods again. "That was the hardest thing that I've ever done. He was selling drugs to children." Logan's fingers touch my hand gently and then entwine with mine. His warmth spreads to comfort me enough so that I can continue. I know that I'm talking to a police detective, but it has somehow become important for me to tell him all of the story. "I naively ignored all the signs, all the little inklings that things weren't as they should be. Alan had a story for every situation, and he was still so confident that everything he said made sense. *I wanted it to make sense.* I didn't look for holes because he was my husband, and I loved him. I trusted that he was telling me the truth. After I was busted with the marijuana in my car, I had to face the facts."

Deep breath. In through my nose and out, slowly, through my mouth. It gives me the strength to continue.

"So one day, I followed him. Alan had ended up with a decent construction supervisor job. His father made sure of that. He was supposed to be working with a crew that was building a new sanctuary for the big Baptist church on the other side of town. But that's not where Alan went that morning. I learned that Alan had been fired about a month before, and I didn't even know."

Logan leans closer. He gently caresses my cheek as I work hard to keep my tears in my eyes. I focus on Logan's eyes and watch him watch me.

"Those boys were so young. They couldn't have been more than seventh graders. My world as I knew it came crashing down that day. Part of me felt dead. I somehow drove to Lilly and Kevin's house. I was so shocked, but you know what, they weren't. Kevin said that he'd been hearing rumors about Alan for a while. He just thought they were rumors though, and neither of them wanted to upset me until they had the facts."

"I confronted Alan that night. I told him what I'd seen. He just gave me excuses about how he lost his job and didn't know how to tell me, and he had to make money somehow to support me."

"Sonovabitch!" Logan exclaims.

"I didn't buy it," I say quickly. "And Alan finally admitted that he'd been using and selling for years. It started while I was away at college. He actually blamed *me* for his illegal activities. He said that if I hadn't *left him* to go to school he wouldn't have gotten into that life. I remember looking at him and not seeing any of the man that I thought I knew. I didn't know my husband, and I don't think I ever did. I tried to be understanding, but then he dropped something that he didn't mean to. In his rant blaming me for everything, he decided to blame me for his affair with Joy. Joy apparently didn't expect anything from him. *She* was more understanding. Once I found out about the affair, I couldn't be understanding anymore. I left him that night, but I didn't turn him in to the police until the next day. After all the promising he did that night about getting clean and starting a new life, he was out on the street selling drugs the very next day. I just couldn't believe it. I thought that we would get him help, some kind of drug rehab, but I followed him again, and he was right back at it."

"Once word got out about Alan's arrest, people decided to come clean about his past exploits. I was so angry, and I felt so foolish. This is a small town. Turns out that lots of people knew that Alan had been fired, and many had heard the rumors about the drugs and Joy and other women. Too many secrets. It was all a lie, almost from the very beginning. I guess it's true that the wife is always the last one to know."

Chapter Thirty

Logan

I can't handle it anymore. I don't want to hear another word about Alan Little. I don't want to hear how much Phoebe loved him, and I don't want to hear about how he hurt her. I wrap my arms around her again and pull her tightly to me. I just want to make it all go away—the pain he caused her and the pain I caused her—all of it gone. I feel her chest rising and falling with my own.

"Phoebe?" She pulls away enough so that she can look into my eyes. "You were right to believe in Alan. He was your husband. It seems to me that you gave him every possible chance until he pushed so far that you had to see him for what he was. Even then, you were strong. Turning him in was not the easy way out. Staying with him and letting everything continue as it was, that would have been the easy way. You did what was right." Maybe my opinion is a little biased, but it makes sense to me.

"I just feel like I ruined his life. I told myself at the time that I turned him in because he was selling drugs to children. It's a good enough reason on its own, but what if I did it because he was cheating on me?

This woman is amazing. Her asshole husband put her through so much, and she still has enough in her heart to make me care about her. How did I become so crazy for her? Almost from the very beginning, I've been thinking about her. I told myself at first that I was worried about her. Well, I *was* worried about her, but it soon became more than that. It quickly became something out of my control, or I never would have visited her. I never would have checked on her, and I never, ever would have slept with her.

"This may sound like a crazy question, but why did you sleep with me?"

Her entire face registers surprise. "What?"

"I know that you're not the kind of woman who sleeps with men you just met. Why did you sleep with *me*?"

The depth of her eyes shows that she's thinking. It's almost as if I can see the currents of blue curling and forming her thoughts. "You make me feel alive." Her voice is husky and full of emotion. "I've been going through the motions since my divorce, just doing the things that I'm supposed to do. But you make me want to *live* again." *Thank you God.* I couldn't have handled seeing regret in those beautiful blue eyes. She places her warm palm against my cheek and holds it there. "Why did you sleep with me? You have a lot more on the line, but you're here."

I place my hand on top of hers. "I haven't been able to get my mind off of you since I walked in your door that night. I was impressed with your strength, even after all you had been through. I couldn't stop thinking about you, and I couldn't stop myself from seeing you—that morning at your sister's house and then that night when Arnie busted me outside. I'm here now, and I don't want to be anywhere else. This is all new for me. I've never felt like this about a woman before, and of all people, she has to be involved in a case that I'm investigating."

Phoebe leans forward, and her lips find mine in one perfect kiss. It's not the rushed, fevered kisses that we've shared before. Instead, it's slow and meaningful and just as full of raw passion. Her hands move to my shoulders, and then she pulls herself up to straddle me. My hands move slowly down her back and then slowly, so slowly, they move down the length of her bare thighs. The heat is overwhelming.

I'm brought back to reality by the ringing of the doorbell. Phoebe sits up. Annoyance and then panic flashes in her eyes. We definitely don't need to be found here together, not like this. She hops off of me and looks around the room. Her hands travel to her mouth and then straighten her shirt. I jump up and stand directly in front of her. I hold her hands in mine until she looks at me.

"It's okay. I'm just here questioning you about the case." She nods.

There's nothing out of place other than the plates of half-eaten pizza and beer bottles. I grab them and quickly head toward the kitchen as she slowly moves to answer the door. I walk up behind her just after she's opened the door.

Alan Little stands on the doorstep.

Chapter Thirty-One

Phoebe

Alan is here.

Right here.

At my house.

He smiles his trademark crooked smile. The one that all us girls used to swoon over. The smile that made him look so innocent as he lied to me.

He never looked *strung out* like the druggies on television, at least not until after I left him and asked for a divorce. Then he let himself go and looked more the part. When he was living with me, he always looked like Alan, and he still does. Obviously, I don't know what drug dealers look like. The only difference now is that he looks a little older than the last time I saw him, and let's face it, so do I. He is more muscular now than he used to be, and I can tell that his body is tight, even through his fitted polo shirt and jeans. His skin looks healthy and tan, probably from working out in the sun in California, if that story is true.

For the record, he doesn't look like a murderer either, but then I'm not sure what a murderer looks like, just like I don't know what a drug dealer looks like.

"What are you doing here?"

"I came to see you." He hands me a bouquet wrapped in green tissue. I reach for the flowers with a shaky hand and pull them to me. They're not flowers. They're a Twizzler bouquet, like the one that Logan gave me. "I was going to come home in July, but I heard what happened. I came home early, so that I can be with you now. So that I can help you get through this." *Huh?* "I've spent the last few years getting my life together, and I want you back, Phoebe." My eyes widen, and I can't help the quick intake of breath that parts my lips. Alan's eyes dart to the side. His smile dissipates, and I know that he's found Logan. "Who the hell are you?" Alan spits.

I'm at a loss, unsure how to proceed. My face is heating up, partly from embarrassment and partly from the anger of Alan taking issue with anyone who is in my home. It's *my* home, not his.

Logan reaches his hand around me to greet Alan. "I'm Detective Logan Matthews. I assume that you've heard about the trouble that happened here last Monday evening. I'm investigating the case and came by to ask Ms. Davidson a few questions." Logan's voice sounds calm and confident. There's no hint that I can see that anything inappropriate was going on between us when the doorbell rang.

"On a Saturday night?" Alan asks snidely. His hands fist together.

"On a Saturday night," Logan replies flatly. He moves to stand next to me. He stands perfectly straight, never taking his eyes off of Alan.

Alan harrumphs. "So, will you be leaving now? I need to speak with my wife."

My shock at seeing Alan has turned to all-out anger. "*I am not your wife.*"

Alan's eyes soften as he looks directly into mine. "This is not turning out as planned. I came here to be with you and to help you. All the way from San Francisco, I might add. I've worked hard to turn my life around, and I want you to be a part of it again. Please, Phoebe, just hear me out. I deserve that much, don't I?"

I need to tread lightly. I don't feel like I'm in danger, not with Logan here. Even if Logan wasn't here, I really don't think that Alan would ever hurt me. I don't think he's capable of killing anyone, especially stabbing someone in my kitchen. Maybe I'm naive for thinking that after all he put me through, but I just can't imagine it.

I look deeply into his light brown eyes. They look clear and aware, not like the hazy eyes of someone stoned. I remind myself that Alan never looked obviously stoned, not in front of me anyway. He was sure to either be off his high by the time school ended, or he went off with his *friends* somewhere so that I wouldn't see him. There was some sloppiness with his stories on occasion, and there were some times that things didn't make sense—those are the times that I shut my eyes tight and didn't see what was right in front of me.

Right in front of me now, I see a man who appears to have his life together, just like he says he does. His light brown hair is neatly trimmed. He looks healthy. His skin is tanned, and his body is fit. He has a small scar on the top of his right cheek near his eye. I wonder if that was from a prison fight. The thought curls my stomach. My eyes find Alan's again. For the first time, there is a hint of uncertainty in them. I'm surprised to see it, but it doesn't matter.

"I'm happy that you've turned your life around. I really am glad to hear it, but I don't have anything else to say to you. Besides the fact that I have moved on with my life, I'm kind of in the middle of being charged with murder right now, and I don't have time to deal with you, too."

"You charged her with murder?" Alan yells at Logan, his eyes wide with disbelief.

"Officially, yes. Ms. Davidson has been charged with murder." Logan somehow keeps his tone official.

"I thought you came here because you knew what happened?" I can't help but ask.

"I heard that a man was stabbed and then died in your house. I didn't know that you were charged with the crime." Alan's kind eyes harden as he turns to Logan. "Phoebe could *never* do anything like that. Are you out of your mind?"

"We are working on some other leads as well," Logan adds quickly.

"Who was murdered?"

"Ron Carpenter," Logan answers, again in his professional tone.

Alan's tan fades about two shades at the mention of Ron Carpenter's name, but his expression remains the same, and he makes no attempt to move.

"Alan, I was just leaving anyway. Detective Matthews is going to give me a ride over to Lilly and Kevin's. I'll be staying there tonight."

"I can give you a ride."

"Why don't you follow us over there, and then you and I can talk?"

Now it's Logan's turn to look surprised. I wish it wasn't written all over his face.

"Do you have everything you need, Ms. Davidson?" Logan asks politely.

"Be right back." I turn and disappear long enough to put the bouquet on the coffee table and grab my purse off the chair in the living room. I'm away from the door for only a matter of seconds, and I'm pretty sure that Logan and Alan spend the time staring each other down.

***

Logan holds the car door open for me. He is absolutely quiet until we are both inside the car. "I don't like this. We were just discussing the possibility that Alan may have *murdered* Ron Carpenter. Now he's here at your house and wants to talk to you? I don't want you speaking with him alone."

"Alan won't *kill* me," I say confidently. I'm pretty sure.

"I'm not going to take that chance. I'm not leaving you alone with him."

"*You have to*. He already thinks it's odd that you were at my house tonight. We don't need to give him any ammunition to use against you. You could get into a lot of trouble. I will be fine at Lilly's. I need to be more worried about Lilly and how she will feel that I'm bringing Alan to her house." Logan stares straight ahead.

I place a quick call to Lilly and give her the news that I'm bringing this craziness to her home. She's just putting the girls down to sleep and turns that task over to Kevin. She isn't thrilled but agrees that I shouldn't be alone with Alan under any circumstances.

I end the call and place my hand carefully on Logan's thigh, so that Alan, driving in the car behind us, won't be able to see the movement. The movement is low, and it's getting pretty dark anyway. I look back behind us and see that Alan is still there, following us closely.

"You don't need to worry. I'm not going back to him...ever. He lied to me for so many years. He could be lying to me right now. He has too many secrets."

Logan's eyes meet mine briefly before they return to the road in front of us. "Everyone has secrets, Phoebe."

I'm taken aback by his words. "I don't. My life is an open book."

He looks at me again, his head cocked to the side.

"I don't," I repeat.

This conversation isn't over, but it's over for now. We have arrived at Lilly and Kevin's. Logan parks on the street, and Alan parks behind us. Lilly is waiting for us on the porch.

"Will you call me later?" I ask. Logan's body tenses.

"I can't call you. There will be a record."

"Why don't you go check out Alan's story, see if he was really on a flight today from California? Then, you can call me later, here at Lilly's and tell me. That's okay, right?"

"I don't want to leave you here with him."

I want to touch Logan to emphasize my point, but I don't dare. Not now. "I will be..." I was going to say *okay*, but Alan has opened my door for me. He smiles down at me and then gives Logan the evil eye.

"Thank you Detective Matthews, for the ride." I smile as warmly as I can. His tight face doesn't change as he stares from me to Alan. I exit the car, leaving Logan no choice but to drive away.

***

Dread fills me as Alan and I walk together toward Lilly's house. Alan's old confidence is back. Does he really think that I'm going to drop everything in my life and go back with him? I couldn't do that. I wouldn't have gone back with Alan even a week ago, before I met Logan. I could never do it now. A small smile forms on my lips as the realization crashes over me. Besides all the other reasons I have to keep Alan out of my life, I only need one—Logan.

I look ahead and focus on Lilly, who has moved to the edge of the porch and now waits for us to make our way to her. Alan greets her with his usual charm. Lilly's expression and body language are reserved. She shakes Alan's hand politely, rather than going for a hug. Lilly is the one who got me through Alan's nightmare. She, more than anyone else, knows what the experience did to me.

Lilly turns and sits down in a nearby wicker chair. Her eyes turn away from us, but I know that she isn't seeing what's in front of her, her focus remains entirely on Alan and me.

I look at Alan, waiting for him to say what he came to say. I don't offer him a seat or invite him in the house. We stand together awkwardly on the porch, under the light, just at the top of the steps. Alan looks at Lilly and then back at me.

"I would really like to speak with you alone."

"You can say anything you need to say in front of Lilly. She won't tell anyone."

Alan brings his hand slowly to my cheek. I turn, and his hand falls away. *I don't want him touching me.*

"Why don't you want to be alone with me?"

"Alan, we are no longer married." I realize that doesn't actually answer his question, but how can I say *I think you might have murdered someone, so I would feel safer with a chaperone*?

"Are you afraid that if we are alone you might believe me, that I might convince you to love me again?"

"No. I don't want to hurt your feelings." Even after all we've been through, I can't believe that I'm being this nice to him. "I'm very happy that you have turned your life around, but I don't want to get back together. I have moved on with my life, and I'm happy."

"Is there someone else? I was told that you haven't dated anyone seriously since I left." Anger begins to fill me, but I quickly clamp it down. Who would have told him that? I don't like it that people are talking about me. This is a small town though, and it's not a secret that I haven't dated anyone. It's the truth.

"I haven't dated much at all," *until very recently*.

"It's the cop, isn't it?"

"No." *Crap.* "Don't be ridiculous." I can't tell if Alan believes me or not.

"I'm not giving up easily. I've been through a lot for you, and I've waited a long time. I can wait a little longer. I will be staying with my parents if you'd like to see me." With that, he turns and walks back to his car. Lilly stands with me on the porch, and we watch Alan drive away together. The hairs on the back of my neck prickle again. Someone out there is watching us.

Chapter Thirty-Two

Logan

I wish that it were as simple as a quick call to the airlines to inquire about Alan's flight status. I do make the call, but after being transferred around to three different people, I end up having to leave a voicemail.

I also call the San Francisco Police Department and start the ball rolling with regard to verifying Alan's story. When I did my search earlier today, I didn't find anything that told me that Alan has been working in California. No driver's license, utility bill, or rental agreement. Nothing. Maybe he pays in cash? Lots of construction work is done under the table. He's driving a Taurus. He would need a valid driver's license and credit card to rent a car. So, how is Alan Little pulling that off? I will wait until

Monday to share this with Swann. I can't risk going overboard on this because of my feelings for Phoebe. If Alan Little is guilty of murder, it needs to stick.

I make my peace with the fact that I want Alan to be guilty. That would be a win-win. It would take the heat off of Phoebe and put my rival away for good. Is that horrible? Probably. I would never frame someone, even Alan, for a crime he didn't commit. I would also never do what Swann has been doing and concentrate solely on Alan. I'm just thinking that it would be awfully convenient all around if he's the murderer. If Alan's guilty of murder, he should go to jail, regardless of whether or not he's in love with the same woman that I am. *Love?* Did I really just have that thought? *Shit.* I am in this deep.

When I can take it no more, I call the Forrester home from my office line. Phoebe answers the phone immediately. "Did you find anything?"

"No. It will take some time, but I'm working on verifying Alan's story."

"You should have called from your cell. That way you wouldn't have had to drive all the way to your office just to make this call." Phoebe's voice pitches up at the end. I can tell that she's smiling. I don't like the sound of this.

"What do you mean?"

"I know that you were watching me again. I understand, but I told you that Alan won't hurt me. Even if I was worried, he wouldn't try anything with Kevin and Lilly here. You didn't have to stay and baby-sit."

I hold my breath. "Did you feel like you were being watched?"

"Yes." Phoebe's word is short, telegraphing her annoyance.

"Did you get that feeling while Alan was there or after he left?"

"Both. That's how I knew it was you. I had thought before that it might have been Alan. It seemed like a long shot at the time, but then he showed up at my house, so it no longer seemed out of the realm of possibility."

"Phoebe, I have been at my desk this whole time." I hear her intake of breath on the other end of the phone. "It isn't me or Alan watching you. It's someone else."

"But, it has to be you." Her tone is now one of almost panic. I have to calm her down.

"This is what we're going to do. I'm going to park around the block and come get you from Lilly's back door. You're going to stay with me tonight."

"I will be safe here."

"You'll be safer with me. Be ready to go in ten minutes."

Chapter Thirty-Three

Phoebe

"It's so romantic," Lilly repeats for at least the tenth time. She's right. It is romantic to be whisked to safety by the hero of my story. It would be a heck of a lot better if I wasn't in danger in the first place.

Someone is watching me. It was creepy enough when I thought it was Logan. Now I know it isn't Logan or Alan. So who could it be?

"Do you love him?"

"I don't know. I don't know if I can love anyone again after all that Alan put me through." Lilly's forehead crinkles in a questioning look. "How do I know if it's love that I'm feeling or just a case of full-on lust? I'm afraid, Lill. I hardly know anything about him, and I've known him less than a week. What if he has things to hide?"

She smiles. "I'm sure he does have something to hide. Everyone does. It's just that most people don't have as much to hide as Alan did. Just follow your heart. You've let your bad experience with Alan control your life for long enough. Let go, and let yourself be in love again."

"But really, what if I'm just in lust?"

"Then enjoy every lustful moment."

Kevin walks into the kitchen to get another beer. He gives Lilly and me a funny look as we stand near the back door giggling together.

"What are you two up to?" he finally asks.

"Phoebe's in love," Lilly says cheerfully, as if that is the answer to everything. It doesn't answer Kevin's question as to what we're *up to,* and it doesn't answer the question of who is following me. It doesn't answer anything, but I know that she believes love is the answer to everything. To herself, she probably makes perfect sense.

Kevin knows that about Lilly, too. He smiles at us both. "So, who's the lucky guy?"

"It's kind of a secret," I answer with a warning in my tone directed right at Lilly. She just smiles as she steps closer to Kevin and snuggles against him. We all share a smile.

A light knock directs our attention to the back door. The light reflects off the glass, preventing us from seeing anyone on the outside. I open the door slowly and find a nervous Logan waiting on the deck. Kevin keeps his arm around Lilly and pulls her toward the door so that he can see too.

Kevin doesn't say a word, bless his heart. He just raises an eyebrow in my direction. I smile and shrug, kiss Lilly on the cheek, and head out the door before Kevin tries to stop me. Lilly is caught up in the romantic aspect of our story. She doesn't want to be bogged down by the irony of Logan and me as a couple or the reality that someone was murdered in my house.

Logan doesn't speak a word. He takes my hand in his and guides me through the backyard. He assists me with scaling their split rail fence, but it's easy. We move around a large shrub, and we're in their neighbor's yard. Logan turns to me suddenly, his lips find mine in a deep kiss. My arms slide around his neck, and my fingers sink into his hair. His hands hug my waist. I feel totally safe in his arms. I don't care where Logan takes me tonight, as long as we're together.

He breaks the kiss and silently pulls me through the yard, around the dark house, and to his car parked on the curb. He starts the engine and entwines his fingers with mine as we drive through the darkness.

***

Logan drives toward the edge of town. I don't ask where we're going. I just trust him to take me there. We pull into the parking lot of the Dairy Queen, and he parks in the back corner of the lot.

"Are you hungry?" I ask him with a smile.

"No. We're going to my apartment, but I don't want to walk you in through the front, just in case someone is watching me, too. I will sneak you in the back and then drive around and park in my usual space. That way everything will look normal. Is that okay with you?"

I nod. I'm excited to see Logan's place. I want to learn more about him. I want to learn *anything* about him. Logan takes my hand in his, and we walk over a grass median that separates the Dairy Queen from one of the two small apartment complexes in our town. This one is made up of a handful of two and three-story walk-ups. I concentrate on the warmth of his fingers as we walk. He slides his thumb lazily over my finger, a tiny movement in the big scheme of things, but it radiates to my toes. Does he know what his touch does to me? I promised myself. No more sex. If this small movement can leave my knees feeling this weak, then my resolve is not looking good.

The night still retains some of the heat of the day, it's a little muggy even. The moon rises above us, full enough that I can make out the silhouette of the man who lives there. It's so very quiet here, just the occasional sound of a car driving by on the main road. It's after eleven, and many of the apartments are dark. This is Hickory Grove. It isn't exactly a hopping night spot.

We walk onto an empty concrete patio. Logan carefully unlocks the door and pulls me inside. The light of the moon is the only light to guide me around an ottoman and coffee table. Logan deposits me carefully onto his couch, kissing me lightly on my cheek.

"It'll take me a few minutes, but I'll be right back. Will you be okay here in the dark?"

"Sure. Just hurry."

"I will. Please don't turn on any lights and don't leave the apartment. I'll only be a few minutes." I watch as he exits through the door we came in, locks it behind him, and jogs across the grass on the way back to his car.

As my eyes adjust to the darkness, I begin to make out some of the items in Logan's apartment: the television, a chair, the bar area that gives a peek into the kitchen. It's such an odd feeling—to sit in a strange place in the dark. I concentrate on Logan's kiss, the one in the bushes of Lilly's neighbor's house. Now that was a kiss, filled with electricity and excitement, and something softer, too.

What's going to happen here tonight? One minute, I tell myself that I can't be with Logan until this mess is cleared up. That's the smart thing to do. But, why should I deny myself time with Logan? He makes me feel incredible. Why should I waste a minute of our time together?

Chapter Thirty-Four

Logan

I jog part of the way back to my car before I realize what I must look like. I'm wearing dress slacks and dress shoes. I bring it down to a fast walk and hurry to my car. It's warm enough that I'm fairly drenched in sweat when I get there. That's fine. I could use a shower anyway.

I drive the short distance around and through the official entrance of the apartment buildings, the one with the sign and perky flowers, and slide into my parking space. A smile is on my lips the entire way. I lock the car and move toward the door. Phoebe is waiting for me in there. Is this what it feels like to arrive home from a long day's work and have someone that you care about waiting for you? It never seemed that appealing to me before. I always thought of a girlfriend—or God forbid, a wife —as an almost literal ball and chain. I finally get it now. This revelation should scare the shit out of me, but somehow it doesn't.

The pain is sudden and intense. It rips through my body as I work to grasp what just happened. I fall forward but keep my balance enough to remain standing.

What the fuck?

I turn quickly, but not in time to miss another punch, this one across my cheek.

There's more than one of them.

What can I see? They're wearing masks. And gloves. Big guys.

I strike out, my punch connects with flesh. I smile with satisfaction.

Another blow, this time to my kidney. Pain radiates through my chest. I suck in a breath, but don't feel the air hit my lungs.

Another hit to my face. There are three of them.

Must fight back. My fist connects again, and then I'm on the ground.

Can't breathe.

The men scatter. A car screeches away.

I lie on the pavement, staring at the blurry moon.

Phoebe.

I roll over slowly and make my way up to a standing position. Hunched over and holding my stomach, I begin to make my way to my apartment.

Must get to Phoebe.

She has to be okay. They were waiting for me. Hopefully they didn't know she was here.

My unsteady feet make the journey. I lunge into the door and hold onto the doorknob and the doorjamb to hold myself up.

Can't get my key in the lock.

"Phoebe? Phoebe, are you okay?" I hear a rustle inside. "It's me. It's okay, but please open the door."

The deadbolt turns and then the doorknob. I fall onto the floor inside my apartment, looking up at Phoebe's panicked face.

"Logan. What happened? Who did this to you?" She looks outside the door and then closes and locks it. There's now light inside, and she's kneeling next to me. Her hands move quickly over my torso and then the rest of me. My arms move around her and pull her down to me.

"Did they hurt you?" My vision begins to tighten, and I can see her more clearly. I pull her even closer. Her hair tickles my nose as I breathe in the scent of her strawberry shampoo.

"Who? Who did this to you?"

"They jumped me. There were three of them."

"We have to get you to a hospital. Or I can call 9-1-1." She jumps up.

"No." I get to my knees and slowly stand. Phoebe's digging through her purse. "I don't want to go to the hospital. It's not as bad as it looks."

Phoebe walks to me. Her gentle fingers cup my chin, turning it toward her. "Let's get you in the bathroom and take a look. You could have a concussion."

She holds onto my elbow and guides me down the hallway, slowly toward the back of the apartment. Guess this is not going to be the romantic night that I was hoping for. My apartment is only a one-bedroom, so it isn't difficult for her to find her way. She walks past the tiny hall bath and into the somewhat larger master bath. She sits me down on the seat of the commode. I squint my eyes to fight off the brightness of the lights and their reflection in the large mirror over the vanity.

Chapter Thirty-Five

Phoebe

Logan's left eye has almost closed. The whole left side of his face is red and swollen. His lip is cut. My shaky fingers work to unbutton his shirt, first down the front and then his cuffs. I remove it as slowly as I can and try my best not to put any pressure on his skin. Next comes his undershirt. I pull it away from his body and work it over his head carefully, again touching as little skin as possible.

Discoloration already marks his right side—pink and lavender, hinting at the heavy bruises to come.

"Oh, Logan." The words are whispers. "Please let me drive you to the hospital." Tears are in my eyes now as I take in his injuries.

"I will be fine. I just need a shower." He stands, bracing the countertop to do so. I kneel down and

204

untie his shoes. He slips them off his feet and then kicks off his pants. His mouth is tight as he tries unsuccessfully not to grimace with each movement. "Just a quick shower, and then I will rest. I promise."

I start the water for him, gather his shoes and clothes, and back out of the bathroom. "Let me know if I can help with anything."

"You can wash my back, maybe whatever else I can't reach." His lips curl into a smile, made crooked by the swelling of his cheek. I return his smile, but it doesn't work as well with the tears falling down my cheeks.

"I don't think that would be the best idea. I'll get you some ice, okay?" He nods. I close the door behind me to give him some privacy and say a silent prayer that he can get into the bathtub without any further injury. *Please let him be okay.*

Logan's bedroom has the normal furniture that you would expect: a bed, a dresser, two nightstands with lamps. That's it. There's nothing personal. No photos. No magazines. Nothing. The only thing on his dresser is a cup, half full of change.

I rummage through the drawers, easily finding a pair of boxers. I peek into the bathroom and set them on the vanity. Logan has made it into the shower. I exhale a prayer of thanks and again leave the bathroom. This time I head for the kitchen. No ice packs in the freezer, but I do find a box of Ziploc bags, so I fill them with ice and make my own.

Logan is sitting on the bed when I return with

the ice packs. He's not wearing the boxers, but has a towel wrapped around him instead. His eyes follow mine as I sit down carefully next to him on the mattress. His chest and back are already showing significant bruising.

"What if you have internal bleeding?"

His hand fits snugly behind my neck. He pulls me to him until our foreheads touch. "I don't have internal bleeding. A concussion maybe, but not internal bleeding." His voice is soft. His breaths mix with my own, leaving me dizzy.

I pull away and look again into his eyes. "It's not funny, Logan. You're hurt. I can't stop thinking that this is my fault. I don't know what I'm involved in, but now you are in it, too. They stabbed Ron Carpenter. What if..."

"No," he says flatly. "I think it was Alan. He was not happy to see us together, so he probably gathered a couple friends to try to teach me a lesson. I would feel the same way if I were in his shoes. Of course, I wouldn't attack a cop, but he's already proven that he's not the smartest guy in town."

"Do you really think it was Alan? He could have killed Ron Carpenter. He could hurt you."

Logan's fingers lightly caress my cheek. "I don't want to talk about Alan. I don't need to go to the hospital. Right now, all I need, Phoebe, is you." Those penetrating eyes echo his words. My breath leaves me in a shudder.

My fingers move lightly over his muscular chest,

which is nothing short of beautiful. My fingers lead the exploration, followed by my lips, as I trail a path of kisses down his hard chest to his tight, flat stomach, careful to avoid his injuries. I push him backwards onto the bed. I already know what it feels like to have him moving inside me, and my body has decided it no longer wants to move slowly. It wants Logan now.

As if he can read my thoughts, a mischievous smile forms on his lips. He takes the hem of my t-shirt between his fingers and lifts it slowly over my head. My hands come together to unclasp my bra, and his hands are there to stop them. He takes each of my hands in his own and pulls me over him. I'm careful not to touch him, afraid to put any weight on his bruised body, but he holds me close. He lazily kisses the swell of my breasts. I wiggle and try to pull away. He chuckles and plants slow and gentle kisses on my bra-covered nipples. Flames pulse through my body, emanating from his lips.

Logan unbuttons my shorts and pushes them down, still in slow, measured movements. I kick them off quickly along with my panties. I don't know how he can stand it.

His touch still elicits the same burning that it did that very first time he touched me. He carefully removes my bra. I move his towel to the side. His hands find my waist and position me on top of him. My eyes are locked with his—so dark and so full of a need that I know is echoed in my own. I feel the tip of him, poised and ready, but he doesn't move. I don't either. Not yet. He caresses my cheek again. And then, when I can take it no longer, I cover him, and he's inside me.

I move slowly at first, unsure of myself. It's been so long. My body remembers what to do. Passion builds with every stroke, our bodies moving together in perfect unison. Logan whispers my name as I explode inside myself, and he follows.

***

We lie together afterwards, but not for long before I make him dress and walk back to the living room. I get Logan settled on the couch with ice packs and brew a pot of coffee. He does have coffee here, even if he usually buys it from the coffee shop. I've heard that concussion victims don't have to stay awake, but I can't just let him fall asleep after being whacked on the noggin like that. It doesn't feel right.

"I'm sorry that this happened to you. Whether it was Alan or someone else, this wouldn't have happened if it weren't for me."

Logan places his hand on my knee and squeezes. "I don't care. I would take this and a lot more to be with you." He takes my hand in both of his. His magic brown eyes study mine and then move over the rest of my face as if memorizing every detail.

I think I'm falling for him. Maybe I've already fallen. How is that even possible when I know so little about his life? I only know how it feels when he touches me. And I know that I trust him. More importantly, I trust myself to let go and just *be* with him.

"Logan, why did you move to Hickory Grove?" This seems like a good place to start.

"I wanted out of Miami." A heavy sigh escapes his lips. "When I was young, I thought that I wanted the big time. I thought that there would never be a dull moment in a city as big as Miami. That is exactly true. There never *was* a down moment. My partner and I worked constantly and never seemed to put a dent in anything. There were always more criminals and more victims. Paul was assigned as my partner as soon as I made detective. He's in his forties, has a wife, and two teenage sons. We clicked immediately. He taught me the ropes, and we learned to trust each other. He's an amazing guy, and we became really close, like the father that I wish I had, instead of the one that I do. He taught me even more respect for the law than I had before, to be a completely straight arrow, follow every rule. That wasn't much of a stretch for me. I've always been on the up-and-up, and that was all good and fine until we found out that one of our co-workers, Sanderson, was taking bribes."

I squeeze his hand tightly. "Paul and I readily agreed that we had to turn him in, and we did. We told the chief. He said he would look into it. The crooked cop was put on a leave of absence, and we thought it was taken care of. A few nights later, Paul and I were following up on a lead on a case we were working, and we were ambushed. They beat the crap out of us and left us for dead. They even ran over Paul's legs as they drove away. It was a miracle that someone found us. They called an ambulance. Somehow we both survived. Paul was on death's door, but the doctors brought him back."

"Oh, Logan." I wipe the tears from my face, only to have them immediately replaced by more. I swallow hard and try to wipe my mind of the image of his partner intentionally being run over.

"I know that Sanderson was behind it, but I could never prove it. He even got his job back. There was no finding against him. The investigation on him turned up nothing—no misconduct of any kind. Word got around that it was Paul and I who turned him in. That didn't make for the best working relationship."

"Why not? The other policemen didn't think you should have turned him in?"

"No. Sanderson was one of the *in-crowd*. He was liked by all, and although I feel he was guilty as sin, he convinced most of the others that I was too much of a narc to be trusted. That I only ratted him out to try to advance my position." I realize my mouth is open and close it. "I kept trying to find something on Sanderson. It was all that I could think about until Paul finally asked me to stop. He could see that I was becoming obsessed. See, after months of being in the hospital and rehab, Paul went home to his family, without his leg. It wasn't just that—he was a changed person after all that he had been through. When it was decided that he could no longer work, I didn't want to work there either." Logan's eyes are now wet as well.

"Paul told me many stories about his first job in a small town in North Carolina where he grew up. I always liked the way it sounded. Crimes obviously happen in small towns, but they're not on the same level as in the cities." Logan sighs. "At least they aren't supposed to be."

I squeeze his hand to let him know that I'm not upset by his gaff. "I looked for openings in small towns on the East Coast. I interviewed here and in Arlington, Maine. I knew Hickory Grove was the place as soon as I saw the ideal little town square and the angled parking spaces for the downtown businesses. Perfect. Well, it would be perfect if it were on the coast so I can fish whenever I want, but the town square makes up for that, at least I thought it did. I walked there the first couple nights after I moved in, but I haven't been back since."

"Maybe we can go there together sometime. Pretty soon, they will start having live music on Friday nights."

"I'll make you a deal. We'll find out who murdered Ron Carpenter, and then I will make you dinner, and we'll attend one of those concerts in public as a date."

I can't help but smile. "That sounds perfect."

"What kind of injuries did you get from the attack? Did it take a long time to recover?"

Logan shakes his head. "A broken arm, a few cracked ribs, and a concussion."

"I'm so sorry."

"Don't be. That's the thing, I didn't have anything compared to Paul. I recovered just fine, and Paul has a prosthetic. It's not fair."

"You can't feel guilty because your injuries weren't as bad as his. You know Paul wouldn't want you to feel that way." Logan's eyes focus downward. "He wouldn't."

"I know that, but now I found you. Why did Paul have to pay so much more for our decision than I did?"

Logan's eyes are so expressive, so kind. They are what drew me to him that very first night. They pulled me out of the grief of finding that man in my kitchen and gave me the strength to answer questions and move forward. Logan's eyes are what pushed me over the edge of my humdrum life and brought me to this very moment.

The corners of my lips tip up into a smile. Logan exhales and smiles as well. He pulls me to him in a tight hug. I hold onto him as if my life depends upon it, and in some ways, it does. I don't want to go back to going through the motions of my life.

I want to live.

He pulls away, caressing my cheek with his

fingertips. He traces my jawline and my lips. My lips part as I lightly kiss his fingers. They are soon replaced with his lips in a slow, gentle kiss. I try to convey how much he means to me in this kiss. I'm not ready to say the words out loud, but I want him to know.

Chapter Thirty-Six

Logan

Phoebe corrals a few stray pieces of hair behind her ear. My chest feels tight as I watch her. She is beautiful. So incredibly beautiful. It's not just physical beauty but her entire being. I can't get enough of being with her. I knew it the moment I entered her house on the night of the murder. I know it now.

"Can I ask you something?" I nod, not sure where this is going, but it can't hurt for Phoebe to ask a question. *I hope.* "Have you ever been married?" *That's an easy answer.*

"No, never have."

"Anyone serious?"

"Not really." I can see her brain begin to work. She eyes me skeptically.

"Why not?" *Not an easy answer*. At least it's not an easy one to tell. I shrug, not sure what to say. I just told her about Paul. I don't need to burden her with all my stories in one night. Or, is it better to pull off the Band-Aid and get this all out of the way. "I won't judge. I married a drug dealer." Her mouth forms a hint of a smile. "I know, I shouldn't have asked. We don't have to talk about it."

"It's okay. I don't want any secrets between us." Big sigh. She looks at me expectantly, mentally bracing herself for my story. I do the same and then begin.

"I've had a few girlfriends, but as soon as they started to get serious, I would make a run for it." Her eyes widen. I can't blame her. I sound like an asshole. Another sigh for me. "I finally figured out that it goes back to my family." I avert my eyes from Phoebe's.

"My father worked wherever he could get a job. He wasn't the most stable provider. He drank too much, so his jobs didn't last. We lived in a little house just outside of Jacksonville. My mother, on the other hand, worked very hard. She was a secretary at an insurance company, and when she wasn't at her job, she was working around the house or working to take care of me. She was the hardest-working person I've ever known." Phoebe brushes my forearm with her thumb, lending me a measure of comfort. I look up to see her understanding eyes but have to look away to continue. She might not be so understanding by the time I get to the end of my story.

"One night when I was five, my father came home drunk. He came home drunk a lot, but this particular night he was angrier than most. He yelled at my mom for not having dinner warmed for him. It was eleven-thirty. She apologized, didn't even stick up for herself, or yell at him for coming home intoxicated. She just started to walk to the kitchen to get his dinner ready. Even at five, I knew that this was wrong. He followed her down the hall, yelling at her, and then shoved her into the bathroom. She grabbed onto the towel rack to stop herself from falling, breaking it off the wall. Then he punched her."

Phoebe's body somehow tenses even more than it already was. She hugs my arm with both of hers and lays her head on my shoulder. I take a few deep breaths and continue. "He broke her nose. Blood splattered all over the place. I had just seen a show on television where they talked about calling 9-1-1. I ran to the phone and started to dial. He pulled it out of the wall before I could complete the call. Mom was begging him not to hurt me and telling me that everything was okay. This was all happening as blood was streaming from her nose. Everything *was not* okay, but I was confused. I knew that what my dad had done was wrong, but he was hugging my mom now and apologizing. They were both crying."

"That's why you didn't use the bathroom anymore?"

"Yeah. I hated that room. I hated that house,

really. I hated my father. Still do. That was the only time that he hit her—that I know of anyway. But, he still made her life a living hell. He left us when I was eight. My brother was only three. My father moved in with some tramp down the street. He didn't even have the decency to move far enough away so that Mom didn't have to see him with his new family. I was happy he was gone, but Mom wasn't. Even after all that he put her through, she wanted him back. She never dated anyone. Nothing. She died when I was twenty. Cancer. She loved him until then."

"I guess I just never wanted to put myself in that position. I never let myself fall in love with anyone. The risk that they could ruin my life is too great. I'd rather be alone." There it is. That's the truth. This is the part where I expect Phoebe to pull away from me, lecture me on the reasons that I shouldn't feel this way. She doesn't. Instead, her arms move around my neck. Her fingers comb through my hair.

She gets it.

There are differences for sure, but she trusted Alan, and he shit on her. I just found it better not to trust anyone—until now. What do I do now?

Chapter Thirty-Seven

Phoebe

"I'm glad that you told me." I smile a huge smile to reassure him. It's more than that, though. I know that this was important to Logan, and he trusts me with it. That means more than I can say. "I wish I had a secret to tell you."

"You have a huge secret. I just already know what it is."

"What?"

"That you're falling for a suave police detective, one that happens to be working on a case you're involved in."

I blush. I didn't realize that I had any secrets, but Logan's right. That's a huge one. "Is another secret that you're the person following me? That you said that you weren't just to get me to spend the night with you?"

Logan shakes his head. "I wish that were true, but I'm not watching you, Phoebe. Not really, anyway. I did sit outside your house for a little while on Friday night, and I followed you to the Carpenter home. I was so worried about you, and I didn't want to take the chance of Arnie shooting me for looking in your windows." I remember how vulnerable Logan looked with Arnie that night and smile. "Are you sure you felt someone watching while Alan was with you?"

"I'm positive."

"Is there anyone that has a grudge against you?"

I think hard about it. "There's really not. I don't want to think that Alan is the killer, but let's say that he is. Say that he stole my house key from my parent's home, then snuck into my house to send the emails, and then killed Ron Carpenter. Would he have had time to drive back to California and then fly back here yesterday?"

"I don't see why not. Swann and I will talk with him on Monday. He'll have to provide his alibi for the time of the emails and the murder." I nod thoughtfully. "Now, given the fact that you're naked and in bed with me, I don't want to talk about Alan anymore."

"We're not naked and in bed. We're dressed and on the couch."

"Only a matter of time." Logan's mouth descends on my neck, and I find I don't want to talk at all.

***

Morning comes too early. It's easy to forget all the bad things when I awaken in Logan's arms, but the reality of our situation is pressing on my chest. Someone killed Ron Carpenter. Someone is trying to frame me for the murder. And it's not just the murder anymore. Now, I'm equally concerned about my relationship with Logan.

Relationship. Is that the correct word to use? What started out as practically a booty call—*me involved in a booty call*—has turned into something much more. It's more for me, anyway. After Logan's admission last night, I have to wonder what this is for him. It was a big deal for him to tell me about his parents. It seems as if he hasn't told that story much, if ever. Does he feel differently about me than the other women he's been with? Am I just kidding myself? He told me that he's never been serious with anyone. My throat feels suddenly tight. If he finds out how I feel about him, will he leave me, too?

Logan stirs, and I turn to face him. The swelling in his face has gone down considerably, just a little left around his eye. It's not black and blue. A dark shade of pink has settled over the left half of his face. His chest is a different story—covered in a purple haze. He should have let me take him to the hospital.

I slide out of bed, dress, and pad to the kitchen. I'm setting up the coffee pot as Logan's strong arms move around me. I turn toward him, and for a long moment, I hold him tightly to me.

***

We repeat the process of last night, only this time I insist on walking to the Dairy Queen alone, while Logan drives around to meet me. Our night together proved that he can handle physical activity, but I don't want him to walk any more than necessary. I'm already wishing that Logan and I could be a normal couple. I don't want to be greedy, but I don't want to say goodbye either.

He drives me down the street to Wal-Mart. We have a plan.

"When will I see you again?" I find I have to ask.

"Probably tomorrow, although I have a feeling it will be with Swann. We need to talk about your email alibis so that we can drop the charges against you. Ask your lawyer to call me, and we'll set up a time to talk. We'll need to talk to Alan tomorrow, too." Logan brings the back of my hand to his mouth and kisses it gently. "I don't know how I'll make it through tomorrow, you know trying to remain *professional*." His lips curve into a smile. A laugh escapes mine.

"Me either, but I'll do my best. You know, they say that if you're nervous, you should picture the other people in their underwear. Would that help?" I bat my eyelashes innocently.

Logan smirks. "That is exactly the problem." His

smile drops, and he turns serious. "I don't know what I might have to say in front of Swann. Please know that I don't mean it, whatever it is."

"I know."

I point out Lilly's minivan in the crowded parking lot, and Logan pulls in to the neighboring parking space. He can't just drive me home or drop me off at Lilly's house. Whoever is watching needs to think that I spent the night there, so we devised this plan to get me back into the house. I will duck as Lilly drives into her garage and no one will be the wiser—hopefully.

I say a quick goodbye to Logan. We had our goodbye kiss before leaving his apartment. We can't afford to have anyone see us together who knows that we shouldn't be. I feel his absence as soon as I close his car door. Lilly's side door is already open, so I duck inside and lie down in the back row.

"I'm going to need *lots* of details when we get home," she announces cheerfully. Turns out that we will not be able to discuss details after all. Hillary and Madison are in full auntie-attack-mode as soon as I walk in the door. I don't mind. There's nothing like having cheers erupt when you walk into a room. That happens to professional athletes and a few other celebrities, but it doesn't happen to normal people. Plus, it gives me a chance to avoid my sister and *not* analyze my relationship with Logan. I don't want to do that right now. I just want to enjoy my floating on clouds moment and not wonder if my clouds are headed for a storm.

My nieces keep me busy until Lilly announces we have one hour until we are expected at Mom and Dad's. Sunday dinner at their house is a family tradition. The girls groan when I stop our card game to get in the shower. Lilly loans me a pair of black shorts and a teal t-shirt to wear, since I'm still wearing the same clothes from yesterday.

"Well?" Her eyes are bright and curious as she looks at me.

"I think it's more than lust. Well, I know that it's more than that for me, and I think that it is for Logan as well."

She grabs me in a tight hug. "Finally. I'm so happy for you." She pulls back enough for me to see her ridiculous grin. "I told Kevin that it doesn't matter that you're dating the cop who arrested you. What matters is that you found each other."

"Unfortunately, it does matter. No one can know where I was last night. Everyone has to think that I spent the night here." Since the only *everyone* who might ask me is Mom and Dad, that won't be a problem.

"I'm so happy for you, Phoebs."

I'm happy for me, too.

Chapter Thirty-Eight

Logan

It's a gorgeous Sunday afternoon. The sun is shining, and although the temperature is high enough to be considered *hot*, I feel great. I know that Phoebe has something to do with my happy mood, probably more than *something*.

Do I dare hope that things will work out between us? That we could have a future together? It doesn't seem out of the realm of possibility. We check out Phoebe's alibis for the times when the emails were written, we drop the charges, and then we can see each other. We can be together without any potential damage to Phoebe or to my career. That could and should all happen tomorrow. *Tomorrow.*

A huge part of me wants to find Alan Little to see if he has a shiner or any other evidence that he's been in a fight. The rational part of my brain makes me stay put. If he has a scratch, that might mean that Alan is responsible for last night. Would I be able to keep my cool and not beat the shit out of him? *Probably not.* Plus, I don't want to do anything that might hamper the Ron Carpenter investigation. If Alan is guilty, I want to make sure he pays for his crime—trying to think of the big picture here.

I can't take the darkness of my apartment any longer. The windows are small and don't let in much light at all. The brightness outside seems to make the rooms darker than they are on a cloudy day.

I walk toward the town square as if I'm being drawn to it. Of course I am. It's the reason that I moved here. It cemented the iconic, small town simplicity that I was looking for to escape Miami's labyrinth. I find the park empty today except for two boys skateboarding along the concrete paths, despite several *no skateboarding* signs. The old me would have chased them away—the old me that never broke any rules. Now look at me. I'm having an intimate relationship with someone that I arrested. Compared to that, skateboarding in the park doesn't seem like a problem at all.

I take a seat on a nearby bench under the shade of a huge Maple tree and dial Paul's number. I've only spoken with him once since I moved here. With everything going on, I have an incredible urge to talk things over with him. I want to tell him about Phoebe, but I don't know if I can. He wouldn't understand. His voicemail greeting plays, and I disconnect. Turns out, I don't have to make that decision today. Paul will see that I called and call me back. I can make my decision when he does.

There isn't much work I can do today. I'm bothered about who could be after Phoebe. Alan? Is Alan guilty of more than attacking me last night? Is he responsible for Ron Carpenter's murder, too? Is he following Phoebe? Maybe I could hang back further and see if I can see anyone else watching Phoebe. I promised her that I wouldn't watch her, and I'm keeping that promise. I'm trying to watch whomever is watching her. That's totally different. At least I tell myself that it is.

Chapter Thirty-Nine

Phoebe

Mom can tell that something is different about me. That's unusual for Mom. She isn't clueless, but growing up, it was pretty easy to keep things from her. Mom has a naive streak in her, so she doesn't go looking for the bad in people. At least I come by it honestly. I'm making it very easy for her today though because I can't seem to wipe the smile off my face. Mom finally gives up asking me and starts interrogating Lilly. Mom hasn't figured out that her attempts to make Lilly talk are useless—Lilly is a steel trap.

We are just sitting down to our ham dinner when the doorbell rings. I look around the table and see my surprise mirrored on the faces around me. Everyone who knows our family, knows that we have a family dinner every Sunday at precisely five o'clock.

"Now who could that be?" Mom asks aloud as she removes the kitchen towel from her shoulder and tosses it on her chair. We watch Mom as she walks toward the front door, all on pins and needles waiting to see whose butt Mom is going to kick for interrupting family time. And then they're all looking at me.

Alan.

He smiles his special smile and hands Mom a huge bouquet of flowers—real ones, not Twizzlers.

"I don't mean to disrupt your family dinner, but I just wanted to come by and see everyone. And well, I knew you would all be here now. I confess that I was hoping that if I happened to *drop by* just before dinner, you might invite me to stay." Alan stops his rambling and looks at Mom. *Is he completely out of his mind?* I stand and walk toward them, but I don't make it in time.

"Of course you can stay," Mom says with manufactured cheeriness. "I could tell that Phoebe was happy about something, but she didn't tell us that you were home." *Ugh*. Mom has given credit for my happiness to Alan instead of Logan. I can't correct her. No one is supposed to know about me and Logan, especially not Alan, of all people. I make way for him to enter, but I don't have to be happy that he's here.

I take a quick moment to look for anything that

might indicate he was responsible for the attack last night. *Nothing*. Alan's face is bruise-free, and his knuckles look fine, too. Logan said that the attackers wore work gloves, so I guess there wouldn't be. Alan is dressed normally, for him at least—khaki pants and a red polo shirt. He gives me a curious glance.

"Mom, Alan probably has better things to do for dinner tonight. I'm sure that his own family would like to spend time with him."

"Actually, they already had plans to attend a dinner party with some friends. They were going to cancel and stay with me, but I told them that I already had plans to come here. I didn't want my surprise visit to inconvenience them. You're not going to leave me with no dinner plans at all, are you?"

"Fine, you can stay." My change of heart has nothing to do with whether or not Alan eats dinner, but I realize that this might actually be a chance for me to find out what he's been up to for the last week. I need to know if he's responsible for Ron Carpenter's death. I feel deep down that Alan is innocent—innocent of committing murder, at least. If I thought he was guilty, I'd never let him in the same house with my family.

I'm hoping that Alan is seated at the opposite end of the table from me, but by the time the shuffling is complete, he has a spot right next to me. Dad says the blessing, and it's chaos for a few minutes as we pile our plates with ham, potato salad, butter beans and biscuits. I pretend that it's Logan sitting next to me. Maybe someday, but probably not. Not when he recently outlined the reasons that he doesn't do commitment.

Lilly sits directly across from me. We make faces at each other when we think no one else is looking. We've learned to convey a lot of meaning with the roll of an eye or the raising of an eyebrow.

"This is just like old times," Alan announces cheerfully. No one agrees with him. The adult members of my family stare at their plates, as if eating suddenly requires concentration. Hillary and Madison take turns throwing curious stares at Alan. He was introduced to them as a friend of the family, but even they can tell that something isn't right.

"So, what have you been doing out in California?" Seems like a good question for me to start with. I can't exactly lead with *where were you at ten o'clock last Monday evening?*

"I work for a few different construction crews. I do drywall work mostly. There's no shortage of building out there. The place is booming. It's cash work, too, so I make a good living."

Alan smiles and stuffs a fork full of butter beans into his mouth. "This sure is delicious, Mrs. Davidson. I haven't forgotten what a great cook you are." Mom beams. I'm sure she hasn't forgiven Alan for what he did to me. Or maybe she has. She's a very Christian woman and believes that everyone deserves a second chance. It's all part of her *believe the best of people* thing. I don't mean to pick on her, it makes her a good person. Dad, on the other hand, is not so forgiving. He wouldn't believe anything that comes from Alan—probably ever. Dad's lip has not uncurled since Alan sat down.

"You didn't have any trouble taking off work to come here?"

Alan lays his fork across his plate and turns toward me. I'm afraid for a moment that he's going to touch me, but he doesn't. He just stares into my eyes. "I had already worked it out with my employers that I would be taking an extended vacation starting next month. When I heard about what happened, I told them that I had to leave early. Family emergency. They were very understanding." *Family emergency, my butt.*

"What happened?" Hillary asks. "What kind of emergency?"

"Nothing to worry about, Pumpkin," Lilly answers. "Nothing to do with our family." Hillary seems appeased and stuffs another piece of ham in her mouth.

"When did you leave California?" I've never been schooled in interrogation techniques. It feels too soon to ask this question, but at the same time, I'm done beating around the bush. If I have to eat dinner with Alan, I want to get something out of it.

"My flight left just after seven yesterday morning. The time change is really against you flying east."

"Did you tell anyone here that you were coming?"

"No. I had told my parents that I would be home on the seventh of July, but I didn't tell them that I was coming home early. I just wanted to get home to you." I choke on my sweet tea. Fortunately, I get myself under control without spitting any out of my mouth. Alan looks around the table. "I owe all of you an apology. I know what a mess I made of Phoebe's life. I was a horrible husband. Heroin is bad news." Lilly grimaces at the word and looks toward her girls. Fortunately, they are focused on their plates and don't seem to be paying us adults any attention. "I've been completely clean for three years. This tea is the strongest substance I've had in a long time. I cleaned up my body, and I cleaned up my life. My love for you, Phoebe, is what got me through the last few years."

The table is completely silent. I'm not surprised by his speech. Lilly and I both heard it last night. I sneak a glance at Lilly. She looks mostly bored, although I think she'd like to ask for someone to pass the potato salad, but she doesn't want to be rude. Kevin lets out a small sigh and begins eating again. Mom's eyes are dreamy, like that is the best declaration of love she's ever heard. She's even smiling. My eyes stop on Dad, at the head of the table. His expression is one of annoyance and disbelief, a stark contrast to Mom's.

Something curls together in the pit of my

stomach. Maybe it's remnants of Mom's lovely dinner, or maybe it's nerves brought on by the craziest week of my life. Whatever it is, it comes together slowly, and then builds upon itself until it's a wave flowing through my body. It becomes more powerful and then shoots out of my mouth as of all things, a laugh. I immediately jump. My hands fly to my mouth, but these feelings will not be silenced. Inappropriate and uncontrollable laughter spews from me, and there's nothing that I can do to stop it.

Alan's hopeful face falls. "I'm...so sorry," I say between breaths. "I don't know...why I'm... doing this. I can't...stop."

Alan pushes his chair back from the table and stands. "I guess that's my cue to leave." He turns to my mother. "Thank you for a lovely meal, Mrs. Davidson. I think I'll be going now."

"Alan, wait." I catch him at the door. He doesn't stop but instead continues outside. "I'm really sorry. I have no idea why I laughed. I swear. I stand by what I said when we talked last night. I don't want to get back together with you. But I'm happy that you're clean and have a chance for future happiness. Everyone deserves to be happy." Alan rolls his eyes and turns away from me. I watch as he skulks to his car and drives away.

"What was that all about, young lady?" Mom is at the door as I walk back inside.

"I don't know what happened. I don't want him back, but I didn't mean to laugh at him."

"Granny, can we have dessert now?" little Madison asks. Tension broken, Mom smiles and walks with Madison to the kitchen. Bless her heart, I love that little girl more than ever.

Chapter Forty

Logan

What the hell was that about? My blood pressure shot to an all-time high when I saw Alan Little arrive at the Davidson's home. He was admitted into the house, and I was a nervous wreck the whole time that he was inside. Why was he here? Was he invited to a family dinner? I push the thought away immediately. There's no way that Phoebe wanted him here. He had to show up on his own. But then Phoebe practically chased after him when he left. My jealousy is getting the best of me, but there has to be a reasonable explanation.

I think about following Alan, but I don't. I stick here with Phoebe. I'm keeping my distance, using binoculars even. So far, I see no signs of anyone watching Phoebe. Are they good enough to be hidden, or are they not here at all?

I follow Lilly and Kevin Forrester's van when they leave an hour later. I assume that they're going either to their own home or to Phoebe's, so I wait a few moments to see if anyone else follows their trail. When nothing happens, I move out.

I try Phoebe's house first and arrive just as she's walking inside. I park as far as away as I can and still see Phoebe's front door. There's no other action on the street. I stay in this spot until after darkness falls. No one visits. Barely anyone even drives down her street. I spend the time vacillating between remembering our night together last night and wondering why Alan was at her parent's house. I think about walking to her back door again. It might be possible to have a repeat performance, but I can't press our luck at not getting caught. So far, we've been foolish and still somehow very lucky to have kept our secret.

***

I'm at my desk before seven o'clock. I could have been here earlier, but the coffee shop doesn't open until six-thirty, and although I could have gone without a good cup of coffee or made my own, I didn't want to miss my opportunity to check out Joy Rogers. She's friendly enough, makes a big fuss about my bruised face. Whatever. I have to say, I would choose Phoebe over Joy any day. I don't see why Alan making the switch was such a surprise to everyone, even Phoebe.

Swann drags in around eight-thirty. He seems a bit on edge. I don't have enough experience with him to know if this behavior is normal or not. Seems like he should be relaxed after a weekend of fishing, but what do I know?

"What the hell happened to you?" he asks, gesturing toward my face. I thought it was looking pretty good, but I guess that's in comparison to Saturday night.

"Three guys jumped me outside my apartment."

"Who were they?" He eyes me skeptically.

"No clue." *I do have a clue. I'm just not telling you.*

"You sure? Did you file a report?" I shake my head. I don't want to talk about my face. My ribs hurt a lot worse, but I don't want to talk about them either. I just want to get on with this day. I try to play it cool, but I'm practically humming on the inside. We need to get the charges against Phoebe dropped as soon as possible. We could have dinner together, tonight. A legit date that we don't have to hide from anyone. I can't do anything about that until her lawyer calls. Hopefully soon.

"I did some work on Saturday. Learned a few things."

"I heard that you visited the Littles. Why did you have to go nosing around without me?" *Nosing around?* This is going to be fun.

"I was gathering information about the case.

Nosing around is my job."

"Why didn't you take the weekend off?"

"I'm new in town, remember? Didn't exactly have a lot to do. I worked all day Saturday. This is a big case. I had the time and didn't want anything to slide."

"What did you find out?"

"For starters, Alan Little is in town. We should question him."

"Maybe. I heard that he flew home *after* he heard that his ex was charged with murder. We have no reason to question him. Not yet, anyway."

My eyebrow raises involuntarily. "Why not? Don't you think his timing is a little suspicious?"

"His story makes sense to me." *Alan's story makes sense and Phoebe's doesn't? What the hell?* "We can make a call to Alan Little's employer, see if he was at work last week."

"I'm already working on that. He doesn't have any hits in California, or anywhere for that matter, since he got out of prison. I have a call into the force in San Francisco to see what they can find out about him. He supposedly has a construction job out there."

Swann nods. "That's what I hear."

"How is it that you are so well-informed about Alan Little?"

"His father called me yesterday. Told me about your visit. Did you learn anything, or was the point to get Mrs. Little all flustered and upset?"

"I just asked them some routine questions. Nothing out of the ordinary. I didn't do anything to upset them."

"Did your work day on Saturday include another talk with Phoebe Davidson?" *I have to tell him that I visited her house. I did it in plain sight. Why did I have to bring the pizza?*

"It did. I visited Ms. Davidson *after* my visit with the Littles. They seem to dislike her very much. They blame her for Alan Little's downfall. I wanted to hear her side of things." *True, just not all of the truth.* Swann eyes me skeptically, but he must decide that I'm being truthful because he doesn't push any further.

"Were you able to get the name of Alan Little's employer? If we had that, then it would make checking his alibi that much easier."

"You've already made a call out there. Let's see what they come up with. If they can't find anything, then we can ask Alan Little for that information."

"I don't understand why you don't want to inconvenience the Littles. These are just questions, perfectly reasonable ones under the circumstances."

"David Little is the mayor of this town, an upstanding citizen. His family has been through some very hard times with all of Alan's antics. I just want to give them some space. If we can find out what we need without bothering them, then that is the way that we will proceed." *Bullshit.*

"Can we at least find out if Alan Little really flew

here from California on Saturday?"

"That, we can do." Swann picks up his phone and makes a call.

***

The call from John Jamison, Phoebe's lawyer, didn't come until almost ten o'clock. The time of the meeting was set for two o'clock, and it seemed like forever before the time arrived. I expel a huge sigh of relief when I see Phoebe and her lawyer exit the elevator.

Finally.

I make eye contact with her lawyer and nod my head in greeting. It takes everything I have not to hold eye contact with Phoebe longer than necessary. I force myself to look across at Swann instead.

"Let's go." It comes out more like a frustrated sigh than actual words. Swann grabs his coffee cup and notebook and heads toward the conference room. I take my time getting my things together. The three of them are seated when I arrive. I take what has become my *usual* seat across from Phoebe and give her a quick hello.

She smiles in return. I think it's just a friendly smile, but it warms my insides just the same. I quickly look to Swann to begin. He's watching me. Did I have a reaction? I think my expression was schooled, but what if he could tell? I look at Phoebe's lawyer. Nothing out of the ordinary on his face.

"It is our belief that in each case someone snuck into Ms. Davidson's home and sent the emails directly from her computer." No reaction from Swann. John Jamison continues, "Ms. Davidson was not at her home at the time that each of the emails was sent. We believe that the killer first stole Ms. Davidson's house key from the home of her parents. The killer then used the stolen key to enter her home each time the emails were sent and then again on the night of the murder."

Mr. Jamison stops and looks at Swann and then me. "Let's go through the emails one by one. The first email was sent on Thursday, June tenth, at 1:43 pm. Ms. Davidson was running errands that afternoon to both the bank and grocery store. She used her debit card to pay for her groceries. The time stamp of her grocery purchase is 2:15 pm. The ATM withdrawal was after that, at 2:27."

I look at Swann and wait for his reaction. I can tell from his expression that this evidence is not good enough.

"That is inconclusive. The grocery store is only five minutes from her home. Ms. Davidson had time to send the email before she left for the grocery store. Is there anyone who can verify the time that she arrived at the store?" Phoebe has no outward reaction to Swann's words, but her shoulders tense.

"Not that I am aware of. We are still looking." Mr. Jamison continues. "The second email was sent on Friday, June eleventh at 12:47 pm. At this time, Ms.

Jamison was having lunch with her friend Melody Griffith at Barney's. I spoke with Ms. Griffith this morning. She stated that they met at Barney's around 12:30 and left just before two. Ms. Griffith would be happy to speak with you to confirm this information."

Much better. Swann nods his head, but doesn't say a word. He looks down the bridge of his nose as if he's thinking. Mr. Jamison sends me a look that says *should I continue?* I shrug and look down at my notes. I don't trust myself to look at Phoebe right now.

"The next email was sent on Saturday at 2:25 pm. Ms. Davidson spent that afternoon at the Winona Country Club swimming pool with her sister and nieces. Ms. Davidson drove first to the Forrester home and then drove with the family to the country club. The pool sign-in log shows that the party arrived at 2:35. Ms. Davidson estimates that she left her home just after two to drive to her sister's house, arriving at approximately 2:10 pm."

We all look at Swann. He simply says, "Continue."

"The next email was sent on Sunday afternoon at 4:59 pm. Ms. Davidson was where she is every Sunday at this time, at a family dinner at her parent's home. She arrived around 4:30. Her parents and sister confirm her story."

"And?" Swann looks angry, but at what I'm not sure.

Mr. Jamison's eyebrow raises, and he continues.

"The last email was sent the day of the murder. Monday at 1:14 pm. Ms. Davidson was visiting her sister at this time. She left home around 1:00 and returned around 2:30. Ms. Forrester can confirm the time estimates, but neither logged the exact times of Ms. Davidson's arrival and departure." Jamison runs through the words quickly. He knows that this one isn't particularly helpful.

"Is that it?" Swann barks. I don't like the smug look on his face. He rubs his chin. "Not one of those is concrete."

"What?" Phoebe practically shouts in disbelief. Her lawyer puts his hand on her shoulder to calm her.

"With the exception of the last one, regarding the email sent on that Monday, each instance shows that Ms. Davidson was not home at the time that the emails were sent."

Swann sighs a heavy sigh. I can't tell if he's actually put out or if he just did it for theatrics. "No, they don't. Let's go through them. Ms. Davidson could have sent the first email *before* she ever left the house to go to the grocery store. The rest rely on the testimony of a friend or her family. There is no denying that Ms. Davidson has a close-knit family. They would cover for her if she needed them to."

Phoebe jumps up. I can't help but look at her now. Besides, it would look odd if I didn't. Her eyes are wide. Her face is bright with anger, not just pink either—full-on red. Her entire neck and face are covered with splotches of varying shades of pissed off.

"My family loves me, but they *would not* lie to the police. *Someone* is trying to frame me for the murder of Ron Carpenter. Would you *please* stop harassing me and find out who the real criminal is?"

"Do you have any theories about who that could be? Who is it that has been so wronged by you, that they would create this elaborate plan for revenge?"

"I don't know." Phoebe takes her seat again, deflated.

"I don't either," he says in a cocky tone. I hold onto the seat of my chair tightly with both hands. I don't want to take the chance that I might punch Swann. "Is there anything else you would like to present at this time? If not, this meeting is over. Thank you for your time." Swann stands regally, reminding me of a peacock showing off his feathers and then walks out of the room.

Phoebe's eyes find mine. They're wet with angry tears. I school my features into a look of indifference. Her lawyer puts his arm over the back of her chair.

"What the hell was that?" he asks me directly. He's frustrated. I can't say that I blame him. I'm frustrated, too. Frustrated that Swann is being such a dick, frustrated that Phoebe isn't off the hook yet, and frustrated that it isn't my arm around Phoebe right now.

Chapter Forty-One

Phoebe

I thought that I'd be walking out of the police station as a free woman. What the heck am I supposed to do now? I need to talk with Logan.

He barely even looked at me.

What's the point of having a boyfriend if he can't be there when I need him? Logan made it clear that he isn't interested in being my *boyfriend*, that he doesn't want a relationship with anyone. It must be awful for him to go through life like that, but it isn't like I could be the one to change him. I'm sure there were those before me who tried, and I've barely known the guy for a week. Just because I've fallen hard doesn't mean it's mutual.

So I'll ask again, what am I supposed to do now? Just wait for him to sneak into my house? *Gosh*. I can't spend another night alone in my house. It doesn't dawn on me again until I'm home and alone. There is someone out there who wants me to go to prison, someone who stabbed Ron Carpenter. Will I meet the same fate? This being brave crap is hard, and I'm really over it.

That's what I wondered about as I lay in bed last night, awake, listening to every nighttime sound of my house and the entire neighborhood for that matter. I finally did doze off, but what a horrible night of sleep. It would have been so much better if Logan had been with me. How long can we go on like this? Crap. I could go to trial. Would a jury convict me based on this evidence? Would they believe that I wasn't home when the emails were sent? Could I actually go to prison? And what about Logan? Do we just keep sneaking around until we get caught? Or, will he think that the risk of getting caught is just too high? Or even worse, will he start to see things Swann's way?

Just when I think things can't get any worse, I find Alan's car parked on the curb in front of my house. *Well, crap.* This is the last thing I need right now.

I walk out to meet him. Arnie and Millie are both watching me out their dining room window. Arnie gives me a nod. *Good.* I feel less alone with them there.

"Can we talk?" Alan asks. He looks at me shyly and then looks at his feet.

I lean back against his car door for support. "What is it, Alan? I think we've done enough talking."

"I just want to try one more time. I've thought only of you these last few years. I love you, Phoebe. I don't understand why you won't give me a chance to show you." I cringe. Yep. This is the last thing I needed today. "Can we go inside and talk about it?"

"Can we talk here?" He takes a step closer, although I don't know why because I've given him no indication that I want him near me. "I'd rather just talk out here."

"Do you ever think you could love me again?" I don't answer, but I guess it's obvious from my non-answer, what my answer is. "Why not? I know that I put you through a lot, Phoebe. I'm clean now. I've always loved you."

"Did you love me when you were screwing Joy? I can forgive the addiction, but I can't forgive the fact that you cheated on me. *For years*. I could never forgive that. You should leave now."

Alan does just that. He does a one-eighty, plops down hard into his car, and drives away. I stand still on the edge of my small lawn and close my eyes. The hot afternoon sun burns my exposed skin. I know that I should go inside, but I don't particularly want to. I don't feel safe inside even though Kevin changed the locks, and the stolen key no longer works.

"You okay, Sweetie?" It's Millie. "Do you want to come over for a little while? I have a brand new bottle of vodka that's just waiting to be opened."

That gets a laugh out of me.

Chapter Forty-Two

Logan

I don't trust myself to speak with Swann right away. Instead, I leave the building. I'm not sure where to go, so I just walk. I'm not surprised when I find myself at the town square. It's deserted in the heat of the day. Makes sense. The heat is stifling. I feel it radiating from the sun and the concrete. I've walked two blocks, and my sweat has already travelled through both my t-shirt and my dress shirt.

I come to no conclusions during my walkabout. If anything, I have more questions, and I'm more frustrated than when I left. Swann's attitude toward Phoebe doesn't make sense. Why is he so focused on her as the suspect?

I find myself nearing the Grove Gazette. I never did meet up with that reporter, Sam Hudson. This is as good a time as any, probably a great time. Not only will air conditioning help my mood, but I might get a different angle to investigate.

The Grove Gazette office is housed in one of the downtown retail spaces like the space we use for the police station but smaller. I quickly surmise that the printing must be done offsite because this Cracker-Jack box is only big enough for a few desks and an office in the back.

The A.C. hits me hard as soon as I open the front door. A middle-aged woman stands to greet me as I enter. She's a little on the heavy side and may appear more so due to her short stature. Her jet-black hair has a sheen of purple that could be brought on from the black dye she used to color it or a reflection of the fabric of her skin-tight dress. She smiles a greeting as she walks around her desk toward me.

I watch her gaze as it travels slowly from my feet up my body until her eyes finally meet mine. I must look worse than I thought I did. No, wait. I don't think it's the sweat she's checking out. I think it's me.

"Welcome to the Grove Gazette," she practically purrs. "How may we help you?" She sticks her chest out a little as her voice rises at the end of the question she just posed. Maybe I should turn and run.

"Will you sit down and finish the copy I just gave you?" A man stands next to her desk. She sighs and plops down, reminding me of a child who can't have another cookie. The man takes a few steps toward me and shakes my hand. "Sam Hudson. What brings you by?"

Sam looks to be about forty. He's a couple inches under six feet tall and stocky. His hair is a very dark brown and cut neatly. The style seems to magnify the thin spots reflecting the light from the top of his head, or it could be the contrast between his very dark hair and very pale scalp. His eyes are dark, but friendly. He's dressed in the same work uniform I am —a dress shirt and slacks, only he doesn't look like he's been walking around town trying to get heatstroke.

"I have a few questions for you. My name is Logan Matthews. I'm..."

He cuts me off, "The new detective. Welcome to Hickory Grove, Detective Matthews. Why don't we go into my office?"

I follow Sam to the back of the room and take a seat in one of the chairs across from his desk. He excuses himself and returns with two glasses of water. I thank him, gulping half of mine in one sip.

"To what do the questions pertain?"

"Alan Little." His curious smile falters a little. He stands and closes the door before returning to his seat.

"Fire away."

"I just want to follow up on a few articles that you've written about Alan. It seems that in the early years, he was praised for his abilities on the football field."

"That's right. He was always good for the perfect feel-good story. He showed some amazing talent on the field. He was a good-looking kid, and his grades were decent enough."

"What happened to him? How did he go from football star to strung-out prisoner?"

"This conversation is *off the record*, yes?" I nod. "I have nothing to back this up. It's just pure conjecture and opinion on my part, but I believe the Littles are to blame." Sam exhales quickly, as if he's just told me a big secret. Of course I wonder *why* he just told me, a complete stranger, this information if he's this nervous about it. But, this is why I'm here.

"How are his parents to blame?"

"Mayor Little has always had a lot of power in this town. His father was also mayor and so was his grandfather. They're one of *those* kind of families. Anyway, David Little thought that Alan was perfect, and he kind of was for a while. I began to wonder about Alan when he didn't go away to college. Who turns down a full scholarship? He was good enough that he might, just might, have been able to go pro someday. He should have at least been dreaming of it. Alan told everyone that he was staying home to be with his girlfriend, Phoebe Davidson. I felt sorry for her at the time, because she took a lot of the blame for his decision."

Sam must notice my surprise because he clarifies. "I don't know if she begged Alan to stay in town or not, but the way I look at it, it was *his* decision, not hers. People calmed down eventually, and most thought that they'd get married. The whole mess started again when *she* decided to go away to school. So, she goes away, and Alan stays around here. His father got him a job with a friend who has a construction business. I always thought there was something fishy going on with him then. Some things just didn't add up. I never really investigated any of it. It wasn't something that I could get away with writing about. It was all based on gossip. That's one thing that this town is good for, lots of gossip."

"What you're saying matches what Mr. and Mrs. Little told me. I don't know the *whys* of the matter, but they are both in the *blame Phoebe* camp." Crap. I have to remember to call her *Ms. Davidson*. Luckily, Sam shows no sign that he noticed.

"Next came the wedding. The Littles didn't like Alan's choice of brides, but they had been together for more than five years at that point, engaged for two. I think the Littles just gave up. They made sure that it was the wedding of the century. They covered the cost of the whole thing. The Davidsons are good people, but they could never have afforded anything so extravagant."

"Things went all right for a couple years, and then everything came crashing down. Alan began using drugs at some point and then selling. No one knows why he did those things. It's one thing to try heroin once and get hooked on it. It's another to deal, especially when you come from the wealthiest family in town. Lots of whys in there."

I nod. "You're right. Lots of whys that I don't have answers to."

"And now we get to the part that explains why I blame Alan's parents. They had to notice that something was going on, maybe as far back as the time when Alan *should have been* in college. I think they ignored the signs, because they didn't want the family name to be tainted with the truth of what their son was. They ignored the problem, but it didn't go away. It only got worse. For a short time, I blamed his wife. She was the closest to him. Didn't she notice what was happening?" *Don't give anything away*. I keep my face locked in the curious expression. "I gave her a pass after she turned Alan in to the police. That took a lot of guts, and I think it was the right thing to do. She made Alan's parents deal with the situation. Of course, they dealt with it by getting a fancy lawyer and getting his sentence reduced, but at least he went to prison for his crimes. She made Alan take responsibility for once, something that his parents never seemed to do."

"How much do the Littles control in this town?"

Sam eyes me skeptically. "Almost everything. If they don't have a direct link, then they know people who do."

I stand and finish the rest of my water. "I appreciate you sharing, but can you tell me *why* you gave me so much negative information about the Littles?"

"During that time, David Little was in my office all the time, trying to censor what I printed in my paper. I didn't have a choice. *Freedom of the Press* sounds great and all, but David Little could close me down in a heartbeat if he wanted to. I never printed a lie or a misleading story. There were a couple stories, though, that I couldn't print at all, and that still pisses me off."

"A newspaper man with integrity. I like that," I say with a smile. "Thanks again. If you think of anything else, please give me a call."

***

My walk back to the station gives me time for a few things to gel. Is Swann giving Alan a pass because of his family? Is it simply that he doesn't want to cross David Little, or has Mr. Little actually requested that Swann stay away from Alan? Maybe Mr. Little is the reason that Swann is so focused on Phoebe. There has to be some reason that Swann isn't questioning Alan, if only to verify his story for elimination purposes.

Swann is at his desk when I return to the office. I feel his scowl as soon as the elevator door opens. I'm pretty sure that the one I'm wearing is similar.

"Where the hell have you been?"

"Thinking. Some things just don't add up for me."

I give Swann another look and decide to just go for it. "Does the reason that we haven't questioned Alan Little have anything to do with the fact that his father is the mayor?"

Swann attempts to steel his features, but I notice his eye twitch. It's minor, but it happens. I sigh heavily. "Is he paying you to put the heat on Phoebe Davidson, or is it a more informal arrangement?" I don't want to be a cocky asshole, but I do have the moral high ground here.

Swann stands. His face reddens. His eyes darken until they're piercing. "She was the most logical suspect. Does the reason that you think she's innocent have anything to do with the fact that you're fucking her?" So much for my moral high ground. "Don't try to deny it. I have pictures."

Shit.

"*You have pictures?*"

"Not of *that*. These." Swann sticks a shaky hand into a brown envelope and comes out with a handful of photos. He hands them to me. A photo of me talking to Phoebe looks back at me. It was taken outside her home on Friday night, after I found her talking with Mrs. Carpenter and followed her home. The next one is me talking to her at her door the next evening with the pizza in my hand. There are others. None of them compromising, but our faces show something more intimate than a detective and witness relationship.

"Did you take these?"

Swann shakes his head. "No. I found them in my car. Someone's been watching you. I just accused you of fucking a suspect, and you don't deny it?" His tone is one of surprise and maybe a little anger. Is he angry about my actions or angry that I'm not defending myself?

"I can't deny it." I say nothing else. I'm not giving him details of my sex life.

"Are you out of your fucking mind? I don't know how you did things down there in Miami, but that kind of behavior isn't going to work in Hickory Grove. You're probably going to lose your job, and she will likely sue our ass off."

"Yes, actually. I think I am out of my mind. I'm confident that she won't sue us, though. I understand that my actions have been extremely inappropriate, and I'm willing to take whatever punishment I have coming to me. This is all on me, though. I guarantee that Ms. Davidson had no ulterior motives."

"How can you be so sure?"

"I'm a good judge of people. She's innocent."

"Huh." I'm not sure which part of my speech has stumped him but count Swann as confused. "I will deny taking money or any other kind of favors from the Littles. I just learned a long time ago that it's best to give them a wide berth for as long as possible. They don't like trouble. But that has ended with the phone call I just received. There's no record of Alan Little taking a flight Saturday or any other day this month."

His words sink in. "What are you waiting for? Find him. Don't let him hurt her."

"Let's go."

"Wait. You want me to go with you? I'm not on probation or fired on the spot or whatever?"

"No. Not yet, anyway. We're short-staffed enough. We'll figure all that out later. We have a murderer to catch." Swann doesn't have to say it twice. We're out the door.

Chapter Forty-Three

Phoebe

I didn't actually drink any vodka at Millie's. I had sweet tea instead. Maybe that was a mistake. It's been one week since I found a man dying in my kitchen. The criminal charges against me *were not* dropped today. Logan will likely not want to be with me anymore. He clearly isn't looking for anything long-term, which might be good, since I might be going to prison. *Crap.*

I don't want to be alone.

I need Lilly.

I need alcohol.

I make a quick call to Lilly and learn that Kevin is working late. No going out for her, so I don't bother telling her why I was calling. Of course she can tell that I'm hiding something, and the questioning begins. I try to act like it's just a call to check in. She doesn't buy it.

"What are you up to? Do you want to come over?"

Do I?

I think of myself drunk and pathetic in her happy home. Ugh.

"No, thanks. I really just wanted to say *hello,* and I have. I'm good now. Thanks Lill." I quickly hang up before she can say another word. I think about my other friends, and as I do, I realize that I don't want to just not be alone, I want to be with Logan. *Crap.* When did it get this bad? When did I fall so hard?

This *relationship* that we have sucks. Am I just supposed to sit around the house waiting for him to sneak in the back door? I can't do that right now. I can't be here alone tonight, and it isn't just because I don't have any alcohol.

I reach for my purse and keys and do something that I've never done before. Go to a bar to drink... alone.

Chapter Forty-Four

Logan

Fortunately, Alan Little himself answers the front door. He sneers when he sees us through the glass, but he schools himself and is all politeness to our faces. He's wearing shorts made of a pastel plaid and a yellow Polo shirt. Not that there's anything wrong with that, but it doesn't say *I work in construction* or *I spent time in prison*. It's just a strange choice for him. Maybe old habits die hard.

I see no evidence that Alan was involved in my beating. He had to be though. I watch him closely. He just gives off the *I'm so innocent* look. It has to be Alan—he's been in prison. He would know to use gloves to cover his tracks. I know that I got a couple good punches in. Maybe his two friends were the recipients.

We sit in the formal living room right off the foyer, the room closest to the front door. Swann and I sit on a velvet-covered couch and Alan on a matching chair. The meeting hasn't started yet, and although there's a tension in the air, we are sitting, which is an improvement from when I spoke with his parents the other day.

Alan makes a big show of looking at his watch. "So, you do put in a lot of hours. It's after six. You work Saturdays and evenings?"

"We work as much as we need to, to get the job done." I know he's just trying to bait me, and it's not going to work. Swann already knows about Phoebe and me, and although we haven't dealt with it yet, it's not something that Alan can hold over my head. Besides, Alan doesn't know for sure that there is anything between Phoebe and me. He's just fishing at this point. Unless he's the one who took the pictures.

"Let's get started," Swann states with authority. It's the first time since I started that I haven't wanted to kick his ass for using that tone. "When did you arrive in town?"

"On Saturday evening. I drove straight to Phoebe's house." He speaks directly to me. I hold his eye contact without worry. This situation would be so much worse if Swann didn't know. I'd be sweating bullets worse than when we talked to Arnie and Millie. Remembering that conversation brings a slight smile to my face. Alan's head tips to the side. "I found this guy with her." Alan gestures toward me with his hand, a satisfied look on his face.

Swann doesn't miss a beat. "Detective Matthews did question Ms. Davidson on Saturday evening. I asked him to."

Alan's eyes practically bug out of his head. "Then he drove her to her sister's house."

"Ms. Davidson asked me to," I say calmly.

"Phoebe and I are getting back together," Alan says smugly. My eyebrow raises. "When you drop the charges against her, and I'm sure that you will, I want you to stay away from her. I don't believe that your intentions are innocent. I saw the way you looked at her. *She's taken.*"

"Mr. Little, can we please get back to the questioning?" Swann interjects. Alan exhales heavily and scoots back into his chair. He nods to Swann. "How did you travel to the area?"

Alan looks down at his lap and sighs. "I've been telling everyone that I flew in from California. I'm not lying to the police, though. It's not worth getting in trouble over." He folds his hands together in his lap. "I was in San Francisco for a while, but I didn't really like it out there. It was too far away from home and Phoebe." His eyes pierce mine briefly—intended to be a warning shot I think. He continues, "I saved up enough money to buy that car. I've been living out of it for the last year, slowly making my way back here. I worked along the way. I was in Charleston, West Virginia when I spoke with my mother. She told me about the man being stabbed in Phoebe's house. I knew I had to get here to help her. That's been my plan all along. Get cleaned up. Get my life together. *Then* go to Phoebe."

"When did you speak with your mother?"

"Wednesday night." Alan removes a piece of paper from his pocket and hands it to Swann. "This is the name of the guy I was working for in Charleston. He can vouch for me being there for the last three weeks. That's what you're here for, right?"

Swann takes the slip of paper from Alan and asks another question. "How is it that you're still so in love with Ms. Davidson when she's the person who turned you in? You went to prison because of her actions."

Alan runs his hand through his hair and then leans forward, resting his elbows on his knees. "Phoebe did the right thing. Sure I was pissed at first, but I wasn't myself then. It was when I stopped using that I realized what a favor she did in turning me in. And I realized what I had lost. I have loved Phoebe from the first time that I talked with her. I lost her once. I can't lose her again." Alan's eyes are wet with tears. His words seem sincere.

My gut wrenches at his words. I can't lose Phoebe either.

"Do you know who might have targeted her?"

"No. Everyone loves Phoebe. Everyone except..." Alan's face pales. "Oh no. No. It's Joy."

"Joy Rogers?" Swann asks. Alan nods, and we're

out the door.

Chapter Forty-Five

Phoebe

I've been to Barney's for dinner countless times, but I've never been to the bar. Sure, I've *sat* at the bar while waiting for a table, but I was always with Lilly or a friend. I've never been here just to be here. This is a whole new experience for me. This week has been just one new experience after another though, so what the heck?

The music is louder on the bar side than on the restaurant side. Guess that makes sense. A U2 classic streams through the room. It's darker over here, too. I stand near the door for a moment to let my vision adjust and scope out the bar. I notice an empty bar stool and walk over to it. The happy hour crowd seems to be winding down, leaving the place with an after-party emptiness. I sit on the backless stool and take a deep breath. I'm here. That wasn't so hard. The bartender is Barney, himself. Barney always reminded me of my dad with his grey hair and stocky, but not fat, build.

"What can I get for you?" *Thank you for not mentioning that I'm drinking alone.* Maybe he thinks I'm meeting somebody here.

"Chardonnay, please."

He smiles. "I don't mean to be rude, but you look like you could use something stronger. How about a rum and Coke, heavy on the rum?" *Geez. Do I really look that bad?* Well, I am here to drink.

"You know what? Why not?"

"Coming right up."

I check out my fellow bar patrons. A few men sit together at the far end. They look tired and ready for a shower. A few other men dot the area. I find the only other woman in the place—Joy Rogers.

Joy tips her drink in my direction. I nod in return. She smiles, steps off her stool, and walks around the bar in my direction. *Oh crap.* I grab the rum and Coke that Barney has just placed in front of me and down half of it before Joy reaches me. She sits on the stool next to me.

"I heard about what happened at your house. Even I think it's ridiculous that *you* were arrested. Everyone knows that you're *too nice* to commit murder." My forehead furrows. Is this a compliment or a jab? Joy has never said anything nice about me —that I'm aware of—so I have to go with the latter.

"What am I supposed to say to that? *Thank you*?"

"Sorry." She smiles sheepishly. "That didn't come out quite right. I guess I'm not used to complimenting you." I take another big gulp of my drink and motion to Barney for another. This conversation is going to take a few more of these.

"I'm sorry, too. I never meant to take Alan from you." Joy's eyes widen. "It's true."

"That's ancient history. Things work out like they do for a reason."

We share a very uncomfortable moment of silence. To break the tension, I ask her the first thing that comes to mind. "Do you have a family?" I already know the answer, but it's all that I could think to ask.

"I have two great kids, boys. Aaron is eight and Brandon is six. I was married, but my husband and I got a divorce just before Brandon was born."

"That sucks, him leaving you before the baby was born. What an ass." Yeah. I should probably stop with the rum. Probably should stop right now. Instead, I take another swig of my fresh drink and push my empty away from me.

"It worked out for the best, actually. He wasn't the right man for me." I nod, like that makes perfect sense and take another sip of my drink. *Rebel Yell* is playing now. I *feel* the drum beat as if it's playing in my soul. Joy's lips are moving, but the drums are so loud that I can't quite make out what she's saying. Maybe I drank too quickly. Mental note—do not down a drink on an empty stomach, or maybe at all —at least until I can practice this drinking in a bar thing. Maybe that's it, I just need more practice.

Joy leans closer to me. "You look like you could use some fresh air." She looks concerned. "I live just down the street. Want to come hang out at my house?"

"Do you have rum?"

She smiles. "Yes, although I'm not sure you need any more."

Why the hell not? I can just add that to my week of firsts. Me hanging out with Joy Rogers. Lilly isn't going to believe this.

"Sure."

***

I'm surprised at how difficult it is to walk after only two drinks. What is two drinks? It must be the two drinks in ten minutes that's the problem. Joy puts her arm around my waist to help support me, to get me to the door.

"Wait. Wait. I know him." I pull Joy toward one of the small tables, near the window.

"Him? I'm sure you don't."

"*I do.*"

"Let's just go." Joy is being nice to me, and I don't want to blow it. So, I wave across the room to Opera Man, my friend from jail. The thought makes me laugh out loud. *I have friends that I made while in lock up.*

The sun isn't gone completely, but it's low enough in the sky that it's behind the buildings as we walk down Main Street.

"This way," Joy says as she pulls me toward the right, and we head down the sidewalk. The disappearance of the sun has already cooled the air dramatically from the heat of the afternoon.

"How much longer? I'm not sure that I feel so well."

I really don't. Each step that I take feels bouncy, like the sidewalk is spongy.

"Why don't we go in here until you feel better?" I look up and realize that she means the coffee shop. It's closed, but she does work here. I nod. Seems like a good idea to me. "My key's for the back door. Come on." I follow Joy around the side of the building and wait while she unlocks the door.

The air suddenly feels too warm. I lean against the back of the building to get my bearings and then vomit on the pavement. I quickly look at Joy, thinking she's going to be pissed, but she has a *I feel sorry for you* face. I feel sorry for me, too.

We enter into a narrow hallway. I follow Joy into a small room to the side that must serve as the office, but there's a couch. I'm overwhelmed with a need to sit down, so I practically fall onto it. The cool air of the coffee shop causes goose bumps to form on my bare arms and legs.

"Feel better?" Joy stands over me with a polite

smile. Whoever knew that she could be so nice?

"Uh huh," I answer softly as I stretch out on the couch and close my eyes.

***

Something isn't right.

I know it before I even open my eyes.

I can't move my arms.

I can't move my legs.

I open my eyes slowly. Both my wrists and ankles are tied together. *What the hell?*

Where am I? Oh yeah. The coffee shop.

Joy.

She stands over me, a smug look on her face. My head is pounding, no longer from the music, but from the effects of the rum and Cokes that I drank and the shock of awaking in this position. My stomach turns.

"What's going on?"

"I'm finally going to get my life back. That's what's going on."

I move myself into a sitting position. Easier said than done in this predicament.

"What?" *What is she talking about?*

Joy turns her body and begins pacing back and forth in the small space in front of the couch. "My life was perfect. *Perfect.* I had the perfect boyfriend, a rich football star. I was homecoming queen and set to be prom queen. Then I'd follow Alan to college, we'd marry and start our life together." I wince. "That's not what happened, is it? Suddenly *you* showed up. Out of nowhere." She stops pacing and stares at me hard before continuing. "I thought it was just a phase, but I was wrong. He wanted *you.* He married *you.* What did you ever do to deserve him?" My buzz is long gone now, leaving me sober enough to know that Joy doesn't actually want answers to these questions.

"You. Don't. Deserve. Him." She pokes me in the shoulder as she spits each word.

"You can have him." I can't help it. I have to say something.

A creepy sort of-psycho smile forms on her face. "I *have* had him." Not sure what my reaction is supposed to be in this situation, so I go with the truth.

"You can keep him."

"Why does he even love you? You left him to go to college. You didn't help him with his drug problem. Instead, what did you do? You turned him over to the police. You sent him to prison." All true, I guess. Plus, I can tell from her maniacal speech that there will be no talking her out of this.

"So, I wanted to send you to prison."

"You." I want to hit her. For the first time in my life, I want to punch someone. I move to stand, but I can't coordinate any clean movements. I can't get my balance with my arms and legs tied together, or maybe it's the left-over effects of the alcohol. Either way, it doesn't work, and I fall, luckily backwards and into a sitting position on the couch. Anger is pumping through my veins like I need it to survive.

"You killed Ron Carpenter? Why?"

"I wanted you to go to prison. For a very long time. You deserve it. You weren't the wife that Alan needed. *I was the wife that Alan needed*. He never would have taken drugs if he had been with me. He would have been a football star. He would have gone pro, and we would live in a big, fancy house, just like his parents."

Joy's eyes now have a dreamy glaze. She plops down in the desk chair a few feet away. Questions begin flowing through my mind.

"You snuck into my house?"

"I did. I knew that the emails had to be sent from your computer for the scenario to be credible. That was the biggest challenge at first, but once I stole the key, it was easy."

Realization hits. "You're the one who's been watching me."

Her face shows no reaction, but then she continues. "I watched at first, so that I could sneak into your house and send the emails. After that, I didn't really need to watch anymore, but I wanted to. I wanted to see you react as your life was falling apart. I loved seeing the police search your house. That was one of my favorites. Was the detective screwing you *before* that? I have to admit that I'm curious about that one."

She seems proud that her plan has come together. Smug even. What is she going to do to me now? She's not going to tell me all this and then let me go. I have to keep her talking.

"I don't *have* Alan anymore. He's in town right now. Why don't you go and tell him how much you love him? Maybe you can start your life together now?"

I feel the sting of her hand as it slaps hard across my cheek. I saw her stand and walk to me. I saw her hand coming toward me, but I couldn't move out of the way. I cry out in pain. She cries out in something. Anguish? She has to be a bit looney toons to have carried out this plan in the first place.

"I told him." Her eyes begin to fill. She eases slowly back into the chair and wipes a tear from her cheek. "I saw him at your house this afternoon, and I know that he's been to see you before. I know you rejected him...again. I thought that this would be my chance. My plan was coming together perfectly. So, I told him. I told him about my baby."

That I wasn't expecting. "What do you mean?"

The smug look is back. "My son Brandon is Alan's. He's the father." A gasp escapes my lips. Joy sits a little straighter in her chair, a satisfied grin on her face. "That's the reason my asshole husband left me. He found out that I was cheating on him." I realize that my mouth is still open and close it, but I can't stop my eyes from bugging out of my head.

Chapter Forty-Six

Logan

Where the hell is Joy Rogers?

We've been to Joy's home, the coffee shop where she works, and Phoebe's home just in case. No one was at any of these places.

Can't find Phoebe either. I've spoken with Lilly. She said that Phoebe called earlier. It was a strange conversation, but nothing that she could really put her finger on. Lilly is calling around to Phoebe's friends and some co-workers, trying to find her. Swann and I are focusing our efforts on finding Joy. We even have the two patrol cars that are working now looking for Joy or her 2001 Ford hatchback.

Swann's phone rings. I can't hear what's being said on the other end of the line. "We'll be right there," Swann states quickly, already turning the car around. "We need to get to Barney's. Bob Hanson saw Phoebe there tonight." He pauses and stares at me. "She left the bar with Joy."

"Why the hell would she do that? She doesn't even like her."

"Bob said that the situation just *felt wrong*. He doesn't know why, but he followed them, and it's been bugging him ever since. He called it in to see if someone could check it out."

I see Bob Hanson up ahead, waiting on the curb in front of Barney's. Swann pulls in next to him, and Bob hops in the car.

"They're at the coffee shop. I saw them go in the back."

Chapter Forty-Seven

Phoebe

"Alan is the father of your son?"

"Yes. We've been together for years." Joy says the words matter-of-factly. They are like a punch in my gut. I knew that Alan cheated on me. I just didn't know or didn't want to think that it was so many times that it was a relationship. I thought it was a now and then kind of thing.

"Does Alan know?" Her face morphs to an all-out snarl.

"He does now. I told him this afternoon, after he left your house. Do you know what he said?" I just look at her. "He said to keep it quiet so that *you* wouldn't find out. Still thinking of you." She stands and begins pacing again. "I told him that you didn't want him. He said that you are just under a lot of stress right now, that you will eventually see how much he loves you. I told him that you were likely going to prison. Do you know what he said? That he would wait for you. You *sent* him to prison and then didn't wait for him. *What the hell is that?* Did you give him a son? *No!* Do you want him? *No!* Why doesn't he want me? Why doesn't he want Brandon?" Tears are streaming down her cheeks. She is on the verge of total meltdown. I don't want to say anything to provoke her further, but I don't know which tact to take.

"You don't need him Joy. You have a good life. You're a mom, and you have a job. Forget about Alan, and find someone who really loves you. You can do so much better."

"I don't want anyone else. Once you're gone, he will *have* to love me." *Oh shit.* I guess I knew that this part was coming. Did she really stab Ron Carpenter? I thought women weren't supposed to kill people in violent ways? We commit suicide with pills. We aren't supposed to use guns and knives. Why is this thought popping into my head right now? I try to push it away to free up enough brain power to think of how to get out of here. What else can I ask her?

"Who was my date that night? Was he in on it, too?"

She looks at me like I'm the one who's lost my mind. "My cousin Stanley," she says dismissively. "He did me a favor." She stands over me and studies me closely. "Don't move. I'll be right back." She leaves the small room and heads in the direction of the front of the shop.

Right. Don't move. I wiggle until I'm sitting on the edge of the couch and then propel myself into a standing position. It's wobbly, but it works. I hop once and then again, and again, and I'm at the hallway. I see the door ahead. Only a few more hops.

I feel myself falling, and then I'm on my back. Joy stands over me, knife in hand. My eyes begin to tear up as much from overall emotion as anger. I kick my legs back toward her. She steps out of the way. She may kill me, but I'm not going easily. Visions of Logan pop into my mind. The varying browns of his eyes. His unsure smile.

Two gunshots fire.

The back door shatters.

I register the look of surprise on Joy's face before she turns and runs toward the front of the store. Someone jumps over me and runs after her.

Logan is with me now.

He kneels down next to me. The sight of him brings me to full-on crying. His arms move around me. His cheek presses against mine.

"Phoebe," he whispers, his breath tickling my ear. He's crying, too.

Noises register from the front of the shop. Logan sits up and then pulls me up to a sitting position. He unties my arms and then my legs. He helps me stand and then pulls me into a tight embrace. The screech of the sirens outside brings me to my senses, and I move away from him. What if Swann saw us like this?

Logan brushes my jaw with his fingertips. "It's okay, Sweetheart. They know. We aren't hiding anymore." His lips move to mine. They're soft and reassuring. Logan breaks our kiss when someone nearby clears his throat. It's Swann. He's holding Joy by the arm, and he's doing something I've never seen him do before. He's smiling.

Chapter Forty-Eight

Logan

We were almost too late. Phoebe is okay. She's here, and she's okay.

Thank you, God.

Fuller and Brown come in through the back door. Fuller's eyes widen when he notices my arm around Phoebe's waist, but he doesn't say a word. He walks to Joy Rogers and begins reading the Miranda. The words sound glorious. I pull Phoebe closer, and we walk outside. I don't even care if I get fired for my inappropriate conduct regarding Phoebe. She's safe, and that's all I care about right now.

Bob Hanson waits nervously by our car. Phoebe smiles when she sees him. "He's the reason we found you. He saw you leave with Joy and followed you."

Phoebe grabs Bob in a tight hug. Bob's pale cheeks turn beet red, a stark contrast to his white hair.

"I guess it's a good thing I ended up in jail after all. If I hadn't, then I wouldn't have met you, and if I hadn't met you, they wouldn't have found me."

That's more than I can take. I pull them both to me.

***

Swann and I drive Phoebe to the station to get her statement. I sit with her in the back and hold her hand. At this point, I've pretty much lost my mind anyway.

Her story is incredible. If I hadn't seen Joy Rogers standing over Phoebe with a knife in her hand, then I would have had a hard time believing that Joy was capable of stabbing Ron Carpenter. Joy planned all of this, set all of this up, for Alan Little. *Alan Little*. He must have really been something back in the day.

"Did Ron Carpenter know Joy?" Swann asks.

Phoebe shrugs. "I don't know."

"I think you've had enough for tonight," Swann finally says to Phoebe. We have been at it for more than two hours. It's almost eleven.

"Detective Swann, please don't blame Logan for what happened between us. It wasn't his fault. Sometimes things happen that are out of our control."

"We will work something out. Why don't you two get out of here?"

"I don't get it. Why the change of heart about me?" I can't wait any longer without knowing the answer.

"I got a call from a Detective Sanderson." My eyebrow raises. "Someone you worked with in Miami?" I nod and wait for him to continue. "He said that you made false charges against someone on the force, and everyone there now hated you for it. That's why you wanted a new job."

"That's not true."

"I know now that I shouldn't have believed him. I should have assumed he had an agenda from the get-go. Truth is, I really wanted Mason to have the job and was pissed that he didn't get it. Sanderson's story just gave me ammunition to justify my dislike for you. And all of that was before I even met you. Now, from what I can see, you're far from the goody-goody that Sanderson accused you of being, and you're smart. You're a good addition to our force."

Swann may work out to be a decent partner after all.

Epilogue

Phoebe

School will soon be starting again. Another summer has come and gone, but this is a summer that I will *never* forget.

It's the summer that Logan found me.

It's the summer that I learned to trust again.

It's the summer that I got my life back.

Logan was suspended for a short time, but he did get to keep his job. It seemed like more of a formality than anything else. Plus, it gave us two weeks to be together. I think of it as catch-up time. The physical part of our relationship started so quickly, and I somehow fell in love with Logan before I even knew him. Now I know him, I trust him, and I love him. I don't have to worry about any of those things.

I proceeded cautiously at first, not wanting to appear too serious, but Logan has never given me any hint of this being too much for him. I no longer worry about him going anywhere.

Logan and I aren't the only love connection to come out of this deal. Bob Hanson, a.k.a. Opera Man, has been spending a lot of time with my neighbor, Mrs. Miller. Turns out that they went to school together and are having a good time getting reacquainted. They both talk a lot about their deceased spouses, but it's nice that they have someone to talk to.

Detective Swann has turned out to be a great partner for Logan. It isn't perfect, but it isn't awful. Logan has been to Barney's with Swann and the guys several times. Mason is even coming around.

Joy Rogers is in jail, without bond, awaiting her trial. I figure she's getting what she has coming to her, but I feel badly for her children. They are being raised by her mother. I've recently met Joy's mother, and she seems like a nice woman and a good grandma. I pray that the kids have a good life with her. It's just a shame that Joy's ex-husband doesn't want to be involved, and apparently my ex doesn't either. Hopefully, the children will never know that.

Alan is gone again. He says to California, but since he lies about so many things, there is no way of knowing for sure. I wish him well. Even if he is a major liar, he is my ex-husband, and I want him to stay clean and be happy.

The town square is pretty crowded tonight. It's the last Friday Night Music Night of the summer. Logan and I have been here together for every one. Together. No longer having to sneak around. Logan comes to my front door now. He parks in my driveway and everything.

Billy Barnes and his bluegrass band are warming up. Logan and I sit together on a blanket, fried chicken shrapnel from our delicious dinner nearby. The sun is low in the sky, casting an orange glow on Logan's face. He smiles, and it radiates from his expressive eyes. This is a moment that I want to remember for the rest of my life.

Logan leans close and whispers in my ear. "I love you, Phoebe." I lean back enough so that I can again see his eyes. "I've never said those words to a woman before, so you know I mean them." I know they're true anyway, even without the words. I see it now, and I've seen it before in his eyes. He cups my chin in his palms. "Marry me."

I nod, smiling from ear to ear. "Yes."

His lips are on mine now, soft and sure and smiling and *mine*. I guess my rule still stands. I only have sex with men who are or will end up to be, my husband.

Dear Reader,

I hope you enjoyed *Perfectly Innocent*. If so, please consider writing an online review. Reviews are very helpful for authors and other readers and would be very much appreciated.

If you would like to be notified of upcoming releases, please sign up for my newsletter at www.tamralassiter.com. I'd also love to connect with you on Twitter or Facebook.

Sincerely,

Tamra Lassiter

Acknowledgements

My sister, Rachel, is a hoot. That's probably what she would say about herself. She's always the life of the party with her witty comments and snorty cackle of a laugh. Thanks Ray for being such a great sister!

Thanks to everyone who helped me make this book a reality. A huge thank you to my writing team: June Kuhne, Rhonda Allen, Anne Newport, Susanne Bhattacharya, Trinh Goettlicher, Peggy Lassiter, and Pat Williams.

Special thanks to Mary McGahren for another amazing cover. I love working with you!

Thanks also to Jena O'Connor of Practical Proofing, Toni Metcalf, and Mary Featherly for your help with editing and proofing.

Thanks always to my husband Brian and our daughters. I couldn't do this without you.

CPSIA information can be obtained at www.ICGtesting.com
Printed in the USA
LVOW11s2201211214

419881LV00005B/277/P